ACCLAIM FOR THE NOVELS OF OPAL CAREW

"A blazing-hot erotic romp . . . a must-read for lovers of erotic romance. A fabulously fun and stupendously steamy read for a cold winter's night. This one's so hot, you might need to wear oven mitts while you're reading it!"
—*Romance Junkies*

4 stars! "Carew's devilish twists and turns keep the emotional pitch of the story moving from sad to suspenseful to sizzling to downright surprising in the end. . . . The plot moves swiftly and satisfyingly."
—*RT Book Reviews*

"Fresh, exciting, and extremely sexual, with characters you'll fall in love with. Absolutely fantastic!"
—*Fresh Fiction*

"The constant and imaginative sexual situations keep the reader's interest, along with likable characters with emotional depth. Be prepared for all manner of coupling, including groups, exhibitionism, voyeurism, and same-sex unions. . . . I recommend *Swing* for the adventuresome who don't mind singeing their senses."
—*Regency Reader*

"Carew pulls off another scorcher. . . . [She] knows how to write a love scene that takes her reader to dizzying heights of pleasure."
—*My Romance Story*

"So much fun to read . . . The story line is fast-paced with wonderful humor."
—*Genre Go Round Reviews*

"A great book . . . Ms. Carew has a wonderful imagination."
—*. . . nce Reviews*

Secret Weapon

Opal Carew

ST. MARTIN'S GRIFFIN

NEW YORK

This is a work of fiction. All of the characters, organizations, and events portrayed
in this novel are either products of the author's imagination or are used fictitiously.

www.stmartins.com

ISBN 978-0-312-67460-1

First Edition: September 2011

10 9 8 7 6 5 4 3 2 1

Acknowledgments

I'd like to give a special thanks to my wonderful editor, Rose, for her patience and enthusiasm for my books, and especially for arranging this wonderful book cover!

Thanks to Emily, my great agent, for inspiring ideas and keeping me on track.

Thanks to Mark and Colette for their love, support and quality assurance.

Thanks to Allie for helping me get unstuck with helpful, creative conversations, for some great ideas for character names, and especially for her warm and generous nature!

One

Sloan Granger hung up his uniform and closed his locker. He was still getting used to life on the police force in the beautiful town of Kenora, Maine. He'd moved here two months ago and didn't regret his decision to leave L.A. at all. It was quieter here and more relaxed, which meant he could focus on more important things than the stresses of the job.

Derek Jameson, still dressed in his own uniform, walked into the locker room.

"Hey, Sloan." He opened his locker a few down from Sloan's, then sat on the flat wooden bench and untied his shoes. "Any big plans for the weekend?"

"Not really. You have something in mind?"

He and Derek had gone out for beers and worked out at the gym a couple of times.

"That depends. Are you seeing anyone right now?"

Sloan raised an eyebrow at the question. "No. I've been too busy settling in." But Sloan knew exactly whom he intended to start dating. Derek didn't know it—none of his new friends did—but Janine was the reason Sloan had chosen to move to Kenora.

Janine and Sloan had history. They'd grown up together and, if things hadn't gotten screwed up because of devastating events, they would be in a relationship right now. But fate had kicked them both in the butt and sent them in different directions. Janine had moved to Kenora six years ago. Mostly to get away from Sloan. He knew that, and he was here to fix it.

"Great. I was wondering if you were free on Friday night."

"Are you trying to fix me up with someone?" Sloan asked. "Because I'm really not interested."

"First, this isn't a fix up . . . exactly . . . and second, if you're not interested in what I'm about to suggest, you need to have your head examined."

Sloan sat down on the bench, too. "Okay, I'll bite. What's on the table?"

Derek leaned toward him. "I go out with this really hot woman and . . . she really likes pushing the envelope, if you know what I mean."

"So you're suggesting what, exactly?" Sloan hadn't been with a woman in quite a while—how could he since all he could do lately was think about Janine? He intended to win Janine's heart, but a wild, no-strings-attached hookup with Derek's woman sounded hot. He had to admit, he was tempted.

"She has this fantasy of having sex with a stranger. We've done it where she's had a blindfold on and we pretend she doesn't know me, but she'd like to try the real thing. I told her I could find someone I trust, and who would be discreet."

"So it would be just her and me?" That would be a bit weird. Making out with a total stranger, knowing she was Derek's girlfriend.

"No, I'll be there. Watching. And getting involved if that seems comfortable once things get started. She'll be blindfolded, at least at first, to heighten the situation. That should make things less awkward, too."

"Sounds like you have this all planned out. You do this a lot?"

"Not the stranger thing. This is the first time. But we've done threesomes before."

"Wow, you've got a really hot one there."

Derek grinned. "Hot in attitude and looks." He pulled his wallet from his pocket and flipped it open to a picture of a beautiful blonde with an angelic smile.

Sloan's heart stopped as he stared at the picture of Janine.

Sloan's heart thundered in his chest as he climbed behind the wheel of his car then sat staring out the windshield at the gray brick wall of the police station.

Derek was dating Janine. Worse, Derek shared her with other men. Sloan's stomach twisted. His sweet, wonderful Janine.

God, she'd always pushed the boundaries as a teen. Staying out late. Trying to get attention from Ben and from Sloan. Of course, she'd always had Sloan's attention, but she had an impish side that required her to torture Sloan as best she could. Or so it had always seemed to him.

Later she always seemed to have a lot of guys around, but he'd never dreamed . . .

She'd never appeared to get serious about anyone. He'd always hoped it was because she was waiting for him. If things had been different . . . If Ben hadn't—

His throat closed and he shook his head, scattering the painful memories before they settled into his mind again, dragging him through hell.

Sloan's hands tightened around the steering wheel. God damn it. Things should have gone differently. She should have been his. If only he hadn't been such an idiot and delayed pursuing a relationship with her for so long.

He started the car and put it into gear, then pulled out of the parking lot and turned left on Jarvis Street. He'd told Derek he'd let him know later. But for God's sake, how could he show up out of the blue as Janine's fantasy stranger? When she saw him, she'd . . .

He turned on Bloomington Street. What would she do? She was an experienced woman, pushing the sexual envelope. She thought nothing of having sex with more than one man at a time, or of having sex, blindfolded, with a total stranger. His fingers tightened around the gearshift as he shifted into fourth.

What would she do if she took off the blindfold and saw Sloan?

His groin tightened at the thought of Janine lying naked beneath him, a blindfold covering her eyes, his swollen cock gliding inside her. He sucked in a deep breath. God, he wanted so badly to make love to her. To experience that with her.

The stranger thing was her fantasy. Would it be so wrong to suggest to Derek that he agree to do the fantasy as long as she kept the blindfold on the whole time? That way she'd never know it was him and he'd get a chance to do what he'd always wanted to do with Janine. Make intense, passionate love to her. Even if she didn't know it was him.

On the other hand, if he didn't do it, Derek would find

someone else, and that thought drove Sloan crazy. He didn't want another man touching her. It was bad enough that Derek made love to her on a regular basis, but some stranger . . .

God damn, the fact that she was in a relationship with Derek . . .

How serious were they? He turned from Bloomington Street onto Carriage Drive, a beautiful tree-lined street of large, stately houses.

Given that they invited other partners into the relationship, he would guess they weren't all that serious. If they were, they wouldn't be looking for excitement outside the relationship.

That meant he just had to wait it out.

Maybe he could find a way to become a regular third in their bed, since she seemed to be okay with that kind of thing. Then when her relationship with Derek waned, Sloan would be right there.

He'd had a chance to have her in his life—to love her and be loved by her—but he'd blown it. Now nothing would stop him from winning her love. He would convince her he was the right man for her, the one to make her happy for the rest of her life.

Somehow he would convince Janine to marry him.

But this Friday night, he would be her fantasy stranger.

"What do you think of this?" Janine stood in the doorway to the kitchen wearing her sexy leather harness, which covered nothing of importance.

Derek's gaze shifted from the newspaper he'd been reading at the kitchen table to her. A wide grin spread across his handsome face, lighting up his chocolate brown eyes. She wanted to run her fingers through his thick, black hair and kiss those full, sexy lips of his.

"Sensational." He stood up and walked toward her, his gaze wandering the length of her body.

He looked incredibly sexy in his dark blue police uniform. Six foot two, thick muscular arms, broad shoulders, and a solid chest. Her nipples rose, tightening, sending tingles through her. He tucked his fingers under the swell of her breast, then lightly stroked her sensitive flesh.

"I can't believe I'm saying this, but I think you should cover these up."

Her eyebrows arched. "Really?"

His hand stroked over her breast, then tweaked her nipple, sending sharp sensations spiraling through her.

"Well, I think it will be too much for my friend all at once." Derek's hand glided down her belly, then cupped her mound. "This, too."

His finger stroked her, then pushed in a little.

She grabbed his tie and tugged him forward, then thrust her tongue into his mouth as their lips merged.

"If you keep doing that"—she sent him a fierce smile as she cupped his balls through his pants and squeezed—"then I'm going to pull out that big cock of yours and fuck you right on the floor."

Derek chuckled and drew his hand from her moistening slit, but she noticed the bulge in his pants had extended. He loved it when she acted aggressive and talked dirty.

"When is your friend coming over?" She unfastened the strap around her neck, then turned her back toward him. "Would you get the snaps at my waist?"

He unfastened them. "Not that I'm complaining, mind you, but you did these up on your own when you put it on."

"Sure. But this is way more fun."

The harness fell away from her body and he handed it to her.

"He should be here in about half an hour."

"Okay." She turned to face him, then ran her fingers over the black leather pouch attached to his belt. "I see you have your handcuffs."

"Yep. I always carry them when I'm with you. Though I don't know why I bother. You have at least two pairs of your own."

"Yeah, but mine aren't real police handcuffs like yours."

"Actually, they are. Except the pink ones." He grinned. "Well, they are, too, but not ones any cop I know would carry around."

She shrugged. "But mine haven't been used by real police to keep people captive." For some reason, the thought that his handcuffs had actually been used to restrain people always turned her on. When Derek snapped them around her wrists, she felt like he was really taking her prisoner.

His brown eyes darkened and he dragged her naked body against his and plundered her mouth. "The thought of my handcuffs is making you hot, isn't it?"

She grinned up at him. "You know it."

"Since you like dating men of authority, you'll love my friend."

Derek hadn't told her the guy's name. That would ruin the game they wanted to play—Janine having sex with a handsome stranger. Derek had assured her his friend was extremely good-looking. Not that it mattered as long as he knew how to treat a woman and liked sex.

Hot, wild sex.

Janine disappeared into the master bedroom and opened her overnight bag. She riffled through the outfits she'd brought, then pulled on a sexy leather bra and thong. Silver chains cascaded from the bra and short links of chains adorned the front of the thong. Anticipation spiked through her as she glanced at the clock. Fifteen more minutes.

She walked down the hall to the second bedroom, where Derek stood waiting for her.

He smiled. "Very nice."

He led her to the wall, where there were sturdy metal loops mounted just above her shoulder height about two and a half feet apart. Metal cuffs dangled from chains attached to the loops. Derek had installed the loops specifically for this kind of play, and when they weren't being used for bondage, he removed the chains and hung candle sconces from them.

He grasped her lower arm and lifted it, then snapped one of the cuffs around her wrist. The feel of the cold steel against her skin sent her hormones dancing. He took her other wrist and fastened the other cuff around it. She stood with her back to the wall, her arms hanging from the cuffs.

He stepped away and smiled. "You look incredibly sexy standing there, totally helpless."

Of course, she wasn't totally helpless. If she told him to release her, she knew he'd do it in an instant, and she had her safe word in case she wanted to stop things anywhere along the way.

Still, she felt helpless. He could touch her any way he wanted. Strip off her clothes. Do whatever he wanted to her, and she couldn't stop him. Not physically.

She had to trust that he'd actually stop if she told him to.

His friend, this stranger she'd never met and whom she wouldn't even see tonight, could do whatever he wanted, too. He would see her. All of her. Naked. Flushed. In the throes of passion. His big hands would caress her. His fingers would slide into her. His cock would fill her.

The doorbell rang.

She sucked in a breath. Oh, God, she was nervous—and extremely turned-on.

"Showtime," Derek said as he slipped the satin eye mask over her face.

The elastic held it firmly in place. She could see nothing.

She heard Derek's footsteps cross the room, then go down the hall. A moment later, she heard the front door open, then two pairs of footsteps retracing Derek's steps.

She could feel the stranger's presence the moment he walked in the room. She didn't know who this man was, but knowing he stood close, looking at her, sent a quiver through her. She stood very still, trying to keep her breathing even.

The total silence dragged on interminably.

Finally, Janine pulled at the chains on the wall. She heard his footsteps as the stranger walked toward her. He stopped and she could feel the heat of his gaze caressing her body. She almost gasped when she felt his hand brush over her shoulder, then graze the tops of her breasts, where they swelled from the black leather bra.

Her skin tingled at his touch, goose bumps dancing across her flesh. Then his hand stroked up her neck and his fingers spiked through her long, straight hair as he cupped her head. She felt his heat as he moved closer. His lips brushed hers and an electric sensation quivered through her.

She hadn't expected him to kiss her. She thought he'd be interested in her only below the neck, but his mouth meshed with hers and his lips moved gently. The tip of his tongue glided along the seam of her mouth and she opened. His tongue slid inside and she met it with hers. They tangled, and he pushed deeper, filling her, his mouth mastering hers.

He released her lips and she sucked in air. God, what a sensational kiss.

His fingers stroked her hair and continued down her chest, stopping above her breast. She waited for the feel of his big hand cupping her, then squeezing, anticipating it with eagerness. His finger dipped between her breasts. He stroked lightly, then his hand enveloped one mound of flesh.

His hand was so hot, so big. Her nipple pushed forward. She longed to feel bare flesh on bare flesh. She arched forward, wanting him to rip the bra from her body and ravage her breasts with his mouth.

"Oh, God, I can't do this," a masculine voice grated.

She froze. *His* voice . . . Oh, God, it couldn't be.

"Sloan?"

Sloan stepped back, away from the lure of her delectable, nearly naked body. Away from the first chance—serious chance—he'd ever had to fulfill his deepest desire to make love to the woman of his dreams. Janine.

He'd wanted her for years. And she'd known it.

When Sloan had called Derek to accept the invitation for

this fantasy night, Derek had clarified that his relationship with Janine was more of a close-friends-with-benefits kind of thing. Apparently, she dated other guys, too. That meant Sloan could actively pursue her, and he fully intended to do so. Hopefully, he hadn't just ruined his chances for good.

Derek unfastened one of her wrists, then the other one as Janine reached for the blindfold. Sloan wanted to flee, but he wouldn't. He always faced his demons. Even a spitfire blonde with the eyes of an angel and the heart of a hellcat.

She tugged the black satin eye mask from her face, revealing those beautiful blue eyes of hers, the same color as the turquoise blue topaz ring on her right ring finger that her brother—and Sloan's best friend—had bought for her graduation day. Now those eyes blazed with emotion, though whether anger or something else he couldn't tell.

"What the hell are you doing here?" she demanded.

Ah, anger.

He grinned, knowing that would throw her off-kilter.

"Is that any way to greet an old friend?"

"Does an old friend try to have sex with me while I'm blindfolded?"

"No, apparently only a stranger can do that."

The sight of her with her hands on her hips and her eyes flashing, especially while she wore that sexy black leather bit of nothing, sent hormones blasting through him. God, he wanted to drag her into his arms and kiss the life out of her.

Next, she would scream at him, and fly into a rage. That would be a sight to see.

But to his surprise, she sucked in a deep breath, calming herself. Her hands dropped to her sides and she drew her shoulders back, standing straight and composed. One would think she wore a tailored business suit and faced someone a rung or two down the corporate ladder rather than wearing a skimpy bit of cloth and facing a man in full police uniform.

"That's the problem with you, Granger. You always find something to criticize."

"I don't criticize. I just want you to be safe." His jaw clenched at her rolling eyes. "For God's sake, Janine. Having sex with a stranger? I could have murdered you."

"Yeah? I don't think Derek would have let you."

She glanced toward Derek, who stood in the background, leaning casually against the wall, his arms crossed and an amused grin on his face.

"Okay, this time, but for all I know, if it hadn't been for Derek, you would have picked up a strange guy in a bar."

Her eyes blazed to life again. "Who the hell do you think you are? Don't judge me."

He held his hands at his sides, palms toward her. "Janine, I'm not judging you. I just worry about you. I want you to be safe."

She sucked in a deep breath. "You sound like Ben."

"Your brother loved you very much. He just wanted you to be careful."

Janine had always been a free spirit. Ben had worried that she was too naïve and that men would take advantage of her. He'd been protective and watchful. A typical older brother.

"Yeah. And ain't it ironic that despite all his urging to be careful and stay safe, that he's the one who's dead now."

The bitterness in her voice showed the depth of pain she still carried at her brother's death.

"He was a cop," he said gently. "It happens."

He saw the pain flash across her blue eyes, but she quickly quelled it.

"Yeah, so I'm told. The point is, life is a crapshoot and I could live my life closed up in a shell, never experience anything, and still get killed crossing the road one day. Or I can simply choose to live my life to the fullest every day." She stepped toward him and poked his chest with her finger. "I choose the latter. And not you or anybody else has anything to say about it."

With that, she turned around and walked away, her sweet ass swaying in a way that made his groin fill with heat. Oh, God, this woman drove him insane.

Janine strode to Derek's bedroom and closed the door, barely blinking back the tears springing to her eyes. She leaned against the door and sucked in a deep breath. She caught her reflection in the mirror. Black studded leather encasing her breasts, the swell of soft flesh pushing over the top, a skimpy black triangle covering her pussy and nothing covering her ass.

Damn, she must have looked like an absolute fool. He thought of her as a bimbo who didn't know what was best for her, and standing there spouting at him, looking like this, would only have accentuated that opinion.

She'd like to think she didn't care, but she did. She'd always respected Sloan, ever since they were kids. Ben and Sloan had been best friends in school, and Janine had always had a bit of a crush on him. Actually, more like a tempestuous, wanting-to-throw-herself-at-his-feet-and-give-him-her-virginity kind of crush. He'd been her first kiss. A kiss that had totally blown her mind and set the bar against which she'd measured every kiss that had come since.

Knowing they were playing with fire, however, they had both backed off. Ben was Sloan's best friend. She was Ben's little sister. If they had continued beyond that kiss, they would never have been able to keep their hands off each other, and there was no way Sloan could have lived with himself if he had defiled his best friend's little sister.

Janine clasped her hands together and her finger automatically found her ring and stroked the blue stone.

After Ben died—shot by some thug during a holdup—Sloan took over Ben's role as her protector. He'd also decided to become a cop. He seemed to thrive on the rules, and on getting some sense of bringing order to the streets, but she wished he could have just been a man—someone to hold her, to help her grieve. Someone to love her and, as much as it rankled her to think it, to take care of her. Not by imposing rules and limitations on her, but by being with her, holding her. Loving her.

After Ben's death, Sloan seemed incapable of touching her. Even at the funeral, when she'd hugged him and cried on his shoulder, he'd stiffened and patted her back, clearly uncomfortable being that close to her. She wasn't stupid. She knew it was probably because he felt it would be a betrayal to Ben. Somewhere along the way, Sloan had equated having sex with Janine to hurting her.

Once Sloan became a full-fledged cop, he'd enlisted his buddies to watch over her, too. It got so that she couldn't turn a corner or talk to a guy without a cop showing up with an eagle eye on her. It made it tough to get a boyfriend.

Finally, she'd left L.A. She needed to find her own way,

needed to get away from Sloan and his overprotectiveness—and her intense yet unfulfilled yearning for him.

Now she had her own gaggle of uniformed men around, but not to protect her. And she'd come to really dig handcuffs.

A knock sounded on the door behind her and she jumped.

"Janine, it's Derek."

She hesitated, her hands balled at her sides.

"Sloan's gone. May I come in?"

She turned and opened the door, then stepped back to let him in. As Derek stared at her, understanding glowing in his warm brown eyes, she feared he saw too much. He drew her against his solid body, and she wrapped her arms around his waist, then rested her head against his chest.

"I didn't know you had a brother. Sloan told me how he died." He tightened his arms around her. "I'm so sorry, sweetheart."

The tears welled, and one escaped and fell on his chest, leaving a damp splotch on his uniform shirt. He stroked her hair behind her ear, then kissed the top of her head.

"If you want to talk about it . . . ."

Ah, damn. She didn't want to dredge up the pain. She didn't want him to see her vulnerability.

"Sure, I'd like to talk." She stroked her hand down his solid washboard stomach, then grabbed the tag of his zipper and tugged it down. She dipped her hand inside and stroked his bulging cock through the cotton of his boxers. "I want to talk about bringing out this bad boy"—she slipped her hand inside his boxers and wrapped her fingers around his swelling erection—"and you shoving me against the wall and driving into me." She squeezed. "Hard."

Two

Janine tugged Derek's uniform pants until they fell to the floor with a thump, then freed his erection from his boxers and stroked its considerable length. Grinning, she stepped back and unfastened her leather bra and eased it slowly from her breasts.

His simmering chocolate eyes watched intently as she drew it downward. She revealed the edges of the aureolas, which were all puckered and nubby, then the tight buds of her nipples. She tossed the garment aside and smiled.

Her fingers found her nipples and she teased them while he watched.

He leaned over and picked up his pants, then retrieved the pouch from his belt. Then he stepped forward and grabbed one of her wrists. Before she knew it, he'd pulled his silver handcuffs from the pouch and flicked one cuff around her wrist. Her breathing caught at the bite of the cold steel and the hard, metallic click as it locked around her wrist.

He turned her around and tugged her hands behind her, then imprisoned the other wrist. His hands gripped her shoulders and he turned her around to face him again.

"I'm sorry, ma'am, but you're under arrest. For indecent exposure."

She grinned at him and nudged her head toward his groin, where his cock stuck straight out of his boxers. "What about you?"

"You're also under arrest for exposing an officer."

She pursed her lips, falling into her role.

"I'm sorry, Officer. I don't want to go to jail. Is there anything I can do to change your mind?"

As he stroked his chin, his gaze dropped to her exposed breasts, which, with her arms cuffed behind her back, arched forward. He grabbed the knot of his tie and eased it down, then pulled it over his head and tossed it away. He stepped toward her, unbuttoning his shirt as he walked, and she stepped back. As she watched him reveal his muscular chest, she felt the bed against her thighs and dropped onto the mattress in a sitting position. He stepped in front of her and stroked his long cock.

"I can think of a couple of things."

With that, he pressed his cock to her mouth. She flicked her tongue out and licked the tip, then opened. He fed his cock-head into her mouth and she closed around him. As she sucked the mushroom-shaped head, he cupped one of her breasts and stroked. He pushed his rod in deeper, her lips stroking his shaft as he glided forward. She opened her throat and he eased deeper still.

His hand stroked her cheek, then cupped her face. He drew back until only half his cock filled her mouth.

"Suck it, baby."

She swished her tongue over the head, then sucked, her cheeks hollowing. She moved up and down on him, speeding up as she heard his raspy breathing accelerate. He groaned and pushed deeper. Knowing he was close, she let him glide from her mouth, then opened her legs wide.

"Are you going to fuck me, Officer?"

He groaned, but quickly pressed his cock to her exposed pussy and nudged her opening. She gasped as he drove forward, impaling her in one, sure stroke. He eased her back, but her hands, still cuffed behind her, got in the way.

"Damn." He put one arm around her waist, positioned the other under her ass, and lifted her.

She wrapped her legs around him as he carried her across the room, his cock jostling inside her, driving her insane with need. Finally, he sat her on the edge of the dresser, then forked his fingers through her long, blond hair and twisted it around his hand. Tilting her face upward, he captured her lips and drove his tongue deep, pillaging her mouth with his forceful strokes.

Still holding her head immobile with his tight hold on her hair, he released her mouth. With their gazes locked, he drew back, then impaled her again. She gasped, her eyelids falling closed.

"Open your eyes." His commanding voice broke through her haze of pleasure.

She opened her eyes and became mesmerized by his heated, intensely sensual gaze. He drew back and drove into her again. Then again. She moaned at the depth of his thrusts. As he pounded into her, her insides quivered. She squeezed him, then gasped as pleasure erupted inside her. He drove deeper, then clutched her body tight to his as he groaned and exploded inside her.

They remained like that, his arms holding her close, as their breathing returned to normal. Finally, he eased back and drew her lips to his, kissing her gently.

He grinned. "You really are a bad girl." He nuzzled the base of her neck, then sucked deeply.

That will leave a mark.

Not that she cared. In fact, it helped remind the other men in her life that she was not exclusive property. Not that any of her current men would protest. She picked them carefully.

Too bad Sloan couldn't be just as cooperative.

Sloan walked toward his car, wondering what the hell he'd been thinking when he'd suggested to Derek that he could take part in that fantasy scenario. Sloan had transferred from L.A. to Kenora knowing Janine lived here, intending to find her and to try to take up where they'd left off when they'd been teens and had discovered the powerful attraction between them.

As he walked past a small corner store, a couple of teenagers leaning against the brick wall noticed him—and the uniform—and straightened up a little, nonchalantly avoiding looking at him. They weren't trouble, he could sense that. Just nervous around authority figures, especially a man with a badge.

When he'd become a cop, hoping to protect the world from thugs like the one who'd taken Ben's life, he'd thrown himself into his work. Only later did he realize he'd had a window of opportunity after Ben's death to be the one Janine leaned on, to allow their relationship to find its way naturally. Not taking advantage of her feelings, but offering her real support. Opening up to each other and becoming close.

But he'd been grieving, too. He hadn't seen what she'd

needed, until it was too late and he'd driven her away. He'd tried to take Ben's place in her life as her protector but missed that she also needed support and compassion.

He'd blown it. She'd moved to Kenora to get away from him, and now he'd stepped into exactly the same role.

What he'd intended was to show her he'd changed. That he could accept her the way she was. Especially now, with her sexual openness and wild lifestyle. If he could convince her he could be a part of it, then he'd win her heart and draw her into a committed relationship.

His first step was to show her he could be just as wild as she could. After this evening, he'd certainly made his job harder.

At the knock on the door Janine glanced up from her magazine. She placed it on the coffee table and walked to the door, then peered out the peephole.

Sloan. Her lips pursed. What was he doing here?

He'd probably come to give her a lecture about last night again.

Well, if he'd come here to lecture, she'd give him a reason to. Annoyed at herself for letting him make her feel guilty, she felt the sudden urge to scandalize him. He knocked again. She took several steps away from the door, unbuttoning her blouse as she went. She slipped it off her shoulders, folded it in half and laid it neatly on the back of the couch, then adjusted the cups of her black lace bra, maximizing visibility of the swell of her breasts. She gazed at her reflection in the glass door of her tall bookshelf. Too bad she wasn't wearing that burgundy bra that barely covered her nipples. Sloan would find that truly scandalous.

He knocked again.

She hurried to the door, and turned the knob. As soon as it unlatched and she pulled it toward her, she said, "Roger, come on in. I'll be ready in a minute."

She almost laughed out loud at the dismayed expression on Sloan's face.

"Sloan. What are you doing here?" she asked innocently.

His gaze raked over her breasts, then he wrenched it to her face, annoyance warring with heated interest in his cobalt blue eyes. Her hormones raged at the fact that he wanted her, despite how much she appalled him. And disappointed him.

She turned her back, walked toward the couch, and retrieved her blouse.

"Do you always answer the door half naked? Without even checking who's there?" he asked.

"Of course not." She slipped her blouse over her shoulders and turned back to face him. "Sometimes I'm completely naked."

Sloan concentrated on breathing, trying to calm the intense anger pulsing through him at her recklessness.

His jaw clenched as he watched her button up her blouse. It didn't help that the sight of her soft round breasts threw his body into an intense state of need. Powerful, conflicting emotions raged through him.

He had to try to make her understand.

"I could have been anyone—"

"Like Roger, whom I'm expecting."

He hesitated. He had slipped in the front door when another tenant exited, so he could avoid using the intercom, just in case she decided not to let him up. It was reasonable that she would assume the knock on the door was this Roger person. Still . . .

"But you didn't know. I could have been some strange man—"

"You are a strange man," she countered.

His nostrils flared. "—who would push in here, slam you against the wall, and overpower you." Exasperated, he emphasized the words in an attempt to impart the seriousness of the situation.

Her lips turned up and her eyes glittered with amusement. "Really? Would you care to demonstrate?"

His jaw clenched and he could feel his vein pulsing at his temple.

"For God's sake, Janine. This is serious."

She rolled her eyes. "Only to you." She finished buttoning her shirt, then leaned against the back of the couch. "Listen, I hate to ask, but what did you come over here to lecture me about *before* you found me answering the door practically naked? Or were you that confident I'd do something to enrage you?"

His lips compressed. Well, he'd blown it again. He doubted she'd listen to his proposition after that. "Could we start over?" he asked. "I came over because I'd like to talk to you about something. I was hoping we could do that now, but if you're expecting a friend, maybe we could do it later."

"Friend?"

"Well, whatever you call your . . . men." Damn, at the tightening of her lips he realized he'd done it again. "I mean, you thought I was someone named Roger. You said you were expecting him."

"Oh, right. Roger." She rocked back against the couch. "Yeah, well . . . I wouldn't worry about that."

Damned little imp. She'd been yanking his chain. He could just throttle her. But then again, maybe he'd deserved it.

"All right. Can we talk now, then?"

She shrugged. "Sure." She stood up and circled the couch, then sat down in the easy chair. "You can grab a beer or a soda from the fridge if you want."

"No, I'm good." He sat on the couch across from her, just wanting to get on with this. He leaned toward her, his hands folded between his knees. "I transferred from L.A to Kenora a little while ago. I've been anxious to look you up, but I wanted to get settled in first, then come and talk to you."

She leaned her chin on her hand. "But then you changed your mind and decided to take part in a sexual fantasy with me? That's an interesting way to contact an old friend."

"That's just it. You and I have never been friends."

A flash of pain slashed across her eyes, totally startling him.

"What I mean is we were always *more* than just friends."

She gazed at him, neither confirming nor denying. Unspoken words hung between them. Damn, it would make it so much easier if he knew what her feelings were about this damnable attraction between them.

Janine's heart thumped. So he admitted there was something between them. If only he could have done that after Ben had died. If only they had acted on their attraction then.

But it never would have worked. They were just so different.

Still, she couldn't help asking the question burning in her mind.

"So when you showed up last night . . . was it a surprise? That it was me. Or did you know beforehand?"

She wouldn't put it past him to pull a stunt like showing up with Derek to teach her a lesson. Catch her red-handed and call her on her behavior.

But then, his kiss still tingled on her lips . . . and his tortured words. *Oh, God, I can't do this,* he'd said. As if he'd really wanted to follow through with the fantasy.

That wasn't the Sloan she knew, though. He wouldn't have sex with a total stranger—if that's what he'd thought she'd be—and certainly not with another man there.

Unless he'd changed more than she knew.

"I knew it was you."

She nodded. So he hadn't changed.

"So you came along just to—"

He held up his hand. "Stop. Before you get all worked up, it wasn't about checking up on you."

"Or criticizing my lifestyle? Or trying to change me?"

He smiled. "Well, if there's anything I've learned in life it's that I can't change you. You are an unstoppable force."

"Why did you do it then?"

"Because I want to have sex with you."

Three

At her widening eyes, Sloan swore to himself. "I mean, I'd like to explore this attraction between us. Start dating. See if things could work out between us."

"And you wanted our first time to be with another man?" She sank back in the chair. "Well, you have changed."

"In fact, I have. Despite getting off to a bit of a rocky start the other night, I wanted to prove to you that I can embrace . . . the wilder side of life."

She raised an eyebrow and her eyes glittered. "Really? Yet you backed off."

"Okay, sure. But that was because I realized I couldn't just have sex with you blindfolded like that."

She grinned. "Got something against blindfolds?"

"No. I mean, you were expecting a stranger, not someone you knew. Not *me*. I realized it would be . . . dishonest. Like I was taking advantage of you."

"And you didn't think of that ahead of time?"

Actually, he had. His conscience had nagged him repeatedly. But his rampant desire to be with her, to feel her soft body wrapped around him, to revel in the sweet heat of her depths surrounding his hard shaft made him lend a deaf ear. He'd *wanted* her. Desperately. He had for years.

"I was afraid you'd turn me down. I thought if I took advantage of the fantasy . . . then you found out it was me . . . you'd agree to keep going with the relationship."

She grinned. "You figure you're that good? Fuck a woman once and she'll want you forever."

He cringed at the rough word, but he knew she was using it just to push him, to see how he'd react. She always tried to keep him off balance. Hell, she always *succeeded* in keeping him off balance.

Now it was his turn. He stared her straight in the eye.

"Actually, yes."

Janine stared into Sloan's piercing blue eyes and felt her composure crack. Under his compelling gaze, she became intensely aware of his strong masculine presence. He was taller than Derek, his shoulders were broader, and his thick, wavy dark brown hair was a little longer. His lips were full and his nose strong and straight. And that square chin of his . . . so sexy. Her insides began to quiver and her breasts swelled. Suddenly, he wasn't her old friend Sloan. He was a strong, vibrant male, all rigid muscle and broad shoulders. Imposing. Authoritative. Powerful.

Oh, God, she could jump him right now.

She gripped the armrests of the chair.

He stood up and stepped toward her, his muscular body lithe and agile. He took her hand and drew her to her feet.

The heat of his body overwhelmed her even before his lips captured hers and she melted against him. His tongue drove past her lips and curled into her mouth, then swirled inside. Her tongue danced forward and curled around his. Her nipples puckered, pushing against his solid chest, and heat washed through her.

Finally, he released her mouth and smiled down at her, obviously confident he'd proven his point.

And he had. He *was* that good. She knew she'd remember that kiss forever. Just like she had their first kiss. And the one last night. If he actually made love to her . . .

She sat down again and he returned to the couch, still smiling.

"I see," she said. "Well, in case you haven't figured it out yet, I'm not really into relationships. At least, not the way you probably mean. I like to be free. I have relationships with several men at a time. They're all casual, and they all understand that I see other people."

"And sometimes more than one at the same time."

She drew her shoulders back and held her head high as she stared into his eyes. "Exactly."

"Okay."

Her heart sank. Was that, *Okay, that means we're dead in the water before we even start* or . . .

"How's Saturday for our first date?" he asked.

"Saturday?" She toyed with her ring, pivoting it back and forth.

This was moving so fast. She needed to get used to the idea of . . . oh, man, having sex with Sloan. It was such a weird concept, yet . . . totally compelling. Especially after that kiss.

Actually, every kiss he's ever given me. There had only been three. Her first kiss ever. The kiss last night. And this one. The first one, there'd been the issues with Ben. The one last night had quickly been followed by his lecturing. Tonight's, though, had opened up a whole new world of possibilities.

She gazed at his intense blue eyes, knowing that despite their powerful chemistry, he'd never be able to accept her type of relationships. Maybe giving him a chance would prove to him once and for all that it would never work between them. Maybe it was the only way she would ever be able to convince him.

"Janine? Is Saturday okay?"

"Sure, Saturday will be fine." She gazed his way. "But I have a few stipulations."

God damn it! The woman always had to have her own way.

Sloan tapped his fingers on his knee as he stared out the back passenger window of the moving car.

Sure, Janine had said she'd come on a date with him, but she wanted Derek and Jonas, a friend of Derek who was visiting from out of town, to join them. It wouldn't be much of a date with those two tagging along, and he sure as hell didn't need chaperones.

Derek, who sat in the front passenger seat, pulled out his cell phone and called Janine when they were about a block from her apartment building. She stood at the front door when they pulled up. Sloan's body tightened at the sight of her in a snug-fitting black dress, which accentuated her curves and was short enough to show most of her incredibly long, shapely legs, augmented by the black spike heels she wore. The strap around her ankles glittered with rhinestones.

Sloan hopped out of the car. "You look sensational."

She smiled. "Thank you."

"You know I would have come up to get you."

She smiled. "That's okay. This is faster."

He ushered her into the backseat and closed the door, then rounded the car, climbed in the other door, and settled in beside her. She set her black wrap and small purse on the seat between them.

Jonas, their designated driver for the night, pulled back onto the road and, fifteen minutes later, they arrived at the tavern Janine had suggested.

Derek opened the tavern door and Janine entered first, followed by Sloan and the others. They settled into chairs at a round wooden table and ordered drinks and nachos. Sloan snagged the seat beside Janine.

"It's nice to see you again, Janine," Jonas said, smiling at her across the table.

Janine smiled back. "You, too."

The waitress returned with a tray of drinks and set them on the table.

Janine leaned toward Sloan. "Jonas is a good friend of Derek's. He comes to town every few weeks or so for a visit. Derek introduced us last time he was here. About a month ago."

Sloan nodded. Had that meeting led to Janine and Jonas having sex? Had both Derek and Jonas made love to Janine at the same time?

The thought troubled him, but at the same time, his cock stirred a little.

"What do you do for a living?" Sloan asked.

"I'm a cop, too. Derek and I worked together until he transferred here two years ago. I've got a sister in town, so now I've got two good reasons to visit."

"He also went through a nasty breakup a few months ago," Derek added, "so I like to do what I can to help him keep his mind off it."

"Like introduce him to me." Janine grinned.

"Well, you do have a way of putting a little excitement into a man's life." Derek sipped his beer from the frosty glass mug in front of him.

"I've heard that," Jonas said, grinning as he gazed at her. "I heard you have something interesting planned for us tonight."

"Derek made the suggestion and I thought it would be a great way to break the ice between us."

"I'm looking forward to it, whatever it is." Jonas' eyes gleamed.

Derek also watched her a little too closely for Sloan's liking.

Sloan had to stop himself from grabbing her hand and dragging her from the table and the two other men showing such intense interest in her.

Damn it, could he really share her with two other men? For fuck sake, he hadn't even been with her himself. Their first time together should not be a shared experience.

Jonas slid his empty mug aside and stood up. "When the waitress comes back, order me another soft drink. I'll be right back."

Jonas headed toward the restrooms, passing the waitress as she returned with a plate of nachos and set them on the center of the table. Derek pointed toward Jonas' empty glass and she nodded and took it with her.

Sloan turned to Janine. "So, have you and Jonas . . . uh . . ."

"No, not yet," Derek answered. "Tonight will be their first time."

Jonas' first time, too? Damn it, Sloan didn't even get to be unique in that tonight.

"Actually, I was a little surprised that you agreed to tonight," Derek said. "After that false start the other night, and then when I found out your history and . . . stuff."

"I'll be fine," Sloan answered stiffly, wondering exactly how much of their history Derek knew. Did he know Sloan had never had sex with her? Did he know they'd been fighting an incredible attraction for more than a decade?

Janine patted Sloan's shoulder. "Sloan tells me he's totally okay with dating on my terms. I think he feels it will add a little excitement to his life."

So she hadn't painted him as a lovesick ex-beau, or worse, a wannabe beau. Instead, it sounded like she'd painted a picture of old friends hooking up for fun and games.

Janine was very aware of Sloan sitting beside her. His closeness. His masculinity. Excitement stirred as she wondered what it would be like when he finally touched her . . . intimately. Kissed her . . . in private places. When they finally stepped over the line they'd drawn in the sand years ago to explore the wild passion they both knew would explode between them.

Jonas returned and sat across from her.

She had to go slowly with Sloan. Walk him through a

few things before going too far. Maybe she shouldn't have set up a date with him tonight, when she'd already committed to a date with Jonas and Derek . . . a date where she and Jonas, who had hit it off wonderfully when they'd met on his last visit, were going to have sex for the first time. She had been looking forward to sex with Jonas ever since the first night she'd met him. Handsome. Sexy. A great sense of humor. And he made her insides tingle.

She absolutely couldn't have sex with Jonas and with Sloan for the first time on the same night. Tonight was about Sloan finding out exactly what going out with her meant. He needed to experience that, to really understand it, before she'd go to the next level with him. She was pretty sure he couldn't handle it, and why put both of them through the heartache if it was never going to work between them?

That's why tonight was actually the perfect night. No matter how tempted she became to have sex with Sloan tonight, the fact that it would be her first time with Jonas would keep things in perspective. She wouldn't diminish the first-time experience for either man. So Sloan could watch, could see what sharing her with other men really meant, but she'd make it clear that she didn't think tonight was the right time for him to participate.

Of course, Jonas wouldn't mind sharing her with other men—that was part of the excitement for him—and he would assume she had been with Sloan before, but Sloan would know. And she would know.

The waitress returned with Jonas' soft drink. Janine sipped her white wine and glanced at Jonas sitting across from her. He was shorter than Derek and Sloan, but had the same broad shoulders and great physique. His dark blond hair was cut short but still long enough to curl a little around his face. When he smiled, his lips turned up a little more on one side than the other, giving him an adorably crooked smile. And she could lose herself in those hazel eyes ringed with dark brown. He glanced at her, caught her staring, and smiled. She almost giggled at the sight of his crooked smile and glowing eyes.

Tonight would be the night with Jonas. And it added a special excitement that Sloan would be there, too. No doubt about it. The evening would be weird but definitely exciting.

"What do you do for fun?" she asked Jonas, then grinned at the gleam in his eyes. "Like hobbies, I mean."

"I volunteer at a local cable company. I used to be part of the stage crew in my high school and enjoyed it, and continued that in college. I missed it after I left school, then found out a lot of jobs at the cable station are volunteer, so I signed up."

"What do you do for them?" she asked.

"Lots of things, really, but usually camera work. That's what I like best. And lighting. What about you?"

"My favorite hobby would have to be reading," she said. "I read a lot and . . . I like to socialize."

Derek chuckled. Sloan grabbed a nacho from the plate in the middle of the table and munched it.

"What about you, Sloan? Any hobbies?" Jonas asked.

"Not really."

That was it. He didn't say any more. Typical Sloan. Didn't reveal himself to anyone. Not even as simple a thing as talking about his interests.

She wondered if he still liked classic cars—or had that been a teenage phase? Did he still enjoy video games? Like going to the movies, especially action/adventure? He'd never shared her passion for books, but she'd always enjoyed going to the movies with him and discussing the story line afterward, usually over burgers and fries at their favorite diner.

She turned her gaze back to Jonas. His gaze slid to the swell of her breasts, accentuated by her deep neckline. Her nipples hardened at the thought that he'd soon be touching her breasts, licking her nipples . . . and more. And so would Derek.

Sloan, on the other hand . . .

Damn, she had to find a way to break it to him—privately—that he would not be participating exactly as he might have hoped this evening.

Four

Sloan followed Janine into Derek's town house, with Jonas and Derek trailing behind. Anxiety gnawed at his insides. How would this work exactly?

"So what is this interesting plan you have for tonight?" Jonas asked as he followed her into the living room.

Janine twirled around and grinned. "I thought it might be fun to play some cards."

"Cards?" It wasn't exactly what Sloan had expected Janine to suggest with three men at her disposal.

"That's right. You like poker, don't you?"

Ah, that's what this was about.

"I'll get the poker chips," Derek said.

Janine draped her wrap over the back of one of Derek's dining room chairs, then sat down. Jonas sat beside her. Realizing that this would probably turn into a game of strip poker, Sloan decided to sit across the table from her. With the round glass dining table, it would be a spectacular view. He gazed at the sexy sight of her long legs crossed at the thighs. Actually, the view was pretty damned hot right now.

Derek returned with a wooden case and set it on the table. He opened it to reveal brightly colored poker chips with white stripes along the edges. He started stacking the casino-quality chips on the table, sorting by denomination. Red at five, green at ten, blue at twenty-five and, finally, black at a hundred.

"Jonas, would you distribute one of each color to everyone while I grab some drinks?" Derek asked.

"Sure." Jonas stood up and began setting out the chips into four equal stacks.

Janine rose. "Sloan, I'm going out on the deck for a minute. Want to join me?"

Sloan stood up and followed her across the living room and out the sliding door onto the back deck, then closed the door behind them. Janine leaned against the railing and stared at the stars glittering above them. Sloan noticed that the cool night air sent goose bumps along Janine's naked arms.

"You're cold. Would you like me to get your wrap?" he offered.

"I'm fine, thanks." She turned to him. "Sloan, I have another request for tonight."

"Really?" He grinned. "You want to neck?"

He stepped closer, ready to draw her into his arms, but she pressed her palm flat against his chest.

"No. In fact, quite the opposite."

Uh-oh. He didn't like the sound of that. "What do you mean?"

"Well, things could get pretty wild tonight."

He shrugged. "That's why I'm here. To prove you can't scare me off. So what's your request?"

"I don't want you to . . . participate in this evening's activities."

"What? You want me to leave?"

"No, I just mean I don't want you and I to have sex tonight."

"But we're playing strip poker?"

"That's right."

"So this is all about getting teased? No follow-through intended?"

He was actually relieved. Being thrown in full force, with two other guys, wasn't his idea of a dream date with Janine.

"Well, for you. But with Derek and Jonas . . . it could go further. I mean, if they want to . . ."

Damn, she was going to strip off her clothes in front of them, then if the other guys *wanted to* she would have sex with them. There was zero chance they wouldn't want to.

"So it's just me being left out? That's not a hell of a lot of fun." He frowned. "So I just sit in the living room while the three of you go off and—"

"Oh, no. You can watch. In fact, I think it's a good idea if you watch."

He grinned. "You want me to watch?"

She nodded.

"While you have sex with two other men?"

She shrugged. "Well, yeah. That's sort of the point. If you can't handle watching—"

"Then you and I are over before we even start." His lips compressed. Damn it, she was testing him. "Look, I told you I can handle it."

"Great. Then there should be no problem."

"Don't you think watching will make it worse, not better? At least, if I'm participating, I'm distracted."

"I'm not trying to make it easier on you."

"Great. Thanks."

"Sloan, if you can't do this, then it'll be clear you can't handle my lifestyle. If that's the case, let's find out right up front. Okay?"

He frowned. "Do I have a choice?"

"You always have a choice."

His eyebrow quirked. "So I can have sex with you to-night?"

"No. I said you have a choice. That's just not one of them."

He glowered. "Fine. We'll do it your way."

She nodded and stepped toward the door, but he grabbed her hand and pulled her against him. He tipped up her chin and gazed into her topaz blue eyes.

"I'm going along with what you want now, but at some point, I'll want some concessions of my own." He stroked her cheek, delighting in the softness of her skin. "And just so you know, sex or no sex tonight, I intend to kiss you." He leaned closer, breathing in her sweet floral yet citrusy scent. "Now. And later."

He captured her soft red lips and drove his tongue between them, tasting her cherry-flavored lip gloss. At first she stiffened, but then she melted against him. He loved the fact she couldn't resist his kisses, even when she was being stubborn. Every time she melted against him, his body hardened in response. Like now. His cock ached with wanting to drive into her.

The sliding door opened. "Hey, you guys. The party's in here," Derek said.

Sloan released her, gazing at her lovely face, her eyes closed. When she opened them, she looked soft and vulnerable. Like a woman who'd just been soundly kissed, and loved it. He wanted to drag her back into his arms and kiss her all over again, but she drew away and headed for the door.

Jonas waited at the table for them. "I thought you'd all abandoned me." He grinned, then took a sip of his beer.

Janine sat down and Sloan took his place across from her. At least he'd be able to enjoy watching her. That was winning right there.

"So how does this work?" Sloan asked. "Why do we have chips if the object of the game has nothing to do with money?"

"Well, the chips don't actually represent money," Derek explained. "They represent the increasing stakes." He picked up one of each color chip. He flicked a red one on the table. "The lowest is Truth. The losing player must answer a question of the winner's choice."

"Is the one with the lowest hand the losing player?" Jonas asked.

"No, everyone who is not the winner has to pay up."

Derek picked up a green chip and tossed it with the others. "Green is Clothing. Self-explanatory. Everyone but the winner removes a piece of clothing. Each player chooses for him or herself what to take off. Two socks count as one item." He glanced at Janine and smiled. "As do stockings."

Derek flicked a blue chip beside the red and green. "Blue represents Dare. This is where the loser must perform some action determined by the winner."

"Wait a minute. What happens if someone folds and the others continue betting?" Jonas asked.

"If someone folds, they have to do whatever action is represented by the last chip they tossed in."

"So if Janine drops out at a green chip, for Clothing, but we all go to Dare, she still has to take something off?" Jonas asked.

"That's right," Derek agreed.

The way Jonas stared at Janine, his gaze lingering on her breasts pushing against the black cloth of her dress, got under Sloan's skin. He didn't like the other man looking at Janine with that hungry look in his eyes, yet at the same time, it kind of turned him on. The thought that Janine would soon strip off her clothes in front of three men, then sit and casually play cards while their hot gazes caressed her body sent his hormones buzzing.

Derek flicked a black chip onto the pile. "Finally, black means Ultimate Dare. With that one, the action is done in privacy with the winner."

"Sounds like fun." Janine stacked her four chips on top of each other, in play order. Red on top down to black on bottom. "I have a suggestion, though. For everything except clothing, why don't we just have the winner choose which player does the Truth or Dare?"

"That's okay with me," Derek said.

Sloan and Jonas both nodded in agreement.

As Derek shuffled the cards, he said, "To keep things simple, we'll draw cards first, then do the betting."

He dealt out the first hand and everyone anted up with a red chip. They all looked at their cards. Sloan had a pair of jacks. Janine discarded two cards, Jonas one. Sloan asked for three new cards, leaving him with the jacks and a king high. Derek took three cards.

Janine, who was to Derek's left, pushed her green chip toward the pot. Jonas did, too.

Images of Janine standing up and stripping off that slinky black dress washed through Sloan's brain. He tossed in his green chip.

"I call," Derek said as he pushed forward his chips, too, then gazed at Janine.

Janine turned over her cards. A pair of queens.

"I can't beat that," declared Jonas.

"Me either," said Derek.

They glanced at Sloan. He couldn't beat it, either, so he shook his head.

Janine leaned back in her chair and grinned. "Okay, boys. Pay up."

All the men unbuttoned their shirts and Janine hungrily glanced around the table at the broad male chests being revealed. As her gaze fell on Sloan's chest, she lingered, sending heat through him.

In the next round, the betting progressed to the same stakes, but Jonas won. More important, Janine lost.

Sloan stripped off his socks as he turned his gaze to her. She stood up and lifted her skirt a little, revealing bare white thigh above the lacy top of her black stocking.

Damn, Sloan wished he'd known she was wearing stockings and a garter belt. He would have fantasized all evening. She tucked a finger under the top of the stocking and ran it around under the lace. He realized there were no garters holding it up. As she rolled the stocking down her long, sexy leg, his cock swelled, pressing painfully against the confines of his jeans. Well, maybe it was a good thing he hadn't known after all.

"I'm not sure that's fair." Jonas grinned as he watched her roll down the second stocking. "We're all naked from the waist up and you're just taking off your stockings."

She smiled. "Don't be a sore winner." She twirled one of her stockings, then crumpled it up and tossed it to him, then did the same with the other one.

"When Janine loses, the winner gets the item of clothing she took off?" Sloan asked. "That's a great bonus."

Jonas stroked one of the stockings against his cheek. "And still warm."

At Jonas' words, Sloan couldn't help thinking about Janine's panties and what it would be like to have her toss them to him, still warm from her body. Possibly damp from excitement.

Janine lost the next round, too, this time to Derek.

Sloan stood up and dropped his pants while Jonas took off his socks. Janine rose and walked over to Derek.

"I need a hand here." She turned her back to him.

He unzipped her dress and she turned around, then lowered it slowly over her shoulders. Sloan's insides heated as the fabric drifted down her chest and over the swell of her breasts. It slipped farther down, revealing her black lacy bra. She pushed the dress over her hips, then released the garment. As it fell around her ankles, Sloan's gaze shifted to the tiny scrap of lace that covered her womanhood. She stepped out of the pool of fabric and leaned over to grab her dress from the floor, which provided Sloan with a great view of her breasts. She handed the garment to Derek.

When she turned and walked back to her chair, Sloan's gaze locked on her perfect, round ass, practically naked except for the tiny triangle of black lace at the top of her thong. His gaze followed her delightfully swaying derriere as she walked back to her chair, then sat down. She crossed her legs and Sloan thanked heaven for his foresight at choosing the seat across from her, giving him a clear view of her entire scantily clad form.

He rested his hand on his boxers, trying to hide his obviously rising erection. The other guys didn't have the same problem yet, since they still had their pants.

Jonas handed Sloan the deck of cards and he realized it was his deal. He shuffled and dealt, keenly aware of Janine's seminude state and her gaze lingering on his boxers.

Betting started with Derek. He pushed forward a green chip. Clothing. Janine glanced at her cards, then matched Derek's green chip. When Jonas also slid forward a green chip without raising, Sloan smiled. He had three sevens, a probable win. He debated whether to raise to a Dare, but right now, more than anything else, he wanted Janine to lose another piece of clothing. When he revealed his hand, the guys groaned. More for effect, he suspected, since all the guys really cared about was whether Janine won or lost. And she'd lost another piece of clothing.

Extremely aware of three intense male gazes watching her, Janine drew in a deep breath as she reached around behind her back and unfastened her bra. Excitement skittered through her at the thought of revealing her naked breasts to these three sexy men.

She dropped one strap over her shoulder, then the other. Under the scrutiny of their hot gazes, she eased the straps off, holding the bra in place. Coyly, she folded one arm over her breasts, then drew the bra downward and dropped it. She covered her breasts with her hands, her arms crossed over her chest.

She leaned back in her chair and smiled at Derek, then Jonas. "Now it's your turn."

Both Jonas and Derek stood up and unzipped their pants, then dropped them to the floor. Both their boxers showed bulges pushing against the thin fabric. The men sat down, but Janine continued to gaze at Jonas through the glass, a smile on her face as she thought about the fact she'd be seeing his erection for the first time very soon.

She glanced at Sloan, anticipating seeing his equipment soon, too. Their gazes locked for a moment and she could see the reflected hunger in his eyes, as though her gaze lit a fire within him. He glanced at the swell of her breasts, pushing above her hands, and she felt heat thrum through her body, too.

Derek slid the deck in front of her.

"Your deal," he said with a grin.

"Actually, it's your deal," she said.

"I'm sure if I take a vote, everyone will agree it should be your deal now."

"That's right," Jonas said.

"I agree," said Sloan.

She laughed. "Okay. I'll deal."

But first, she pressed her hands more tightly over her breasts and squeezed them, to murmurs of approval from the men. Then she glided her fingers over her distended nipples, basking in the glinting need in their eyes. She released her breasts, exposing them for the first time, then picked up the cards and shuffled. As she dealt the hands, her breasts ached with the heat of their intense scrutiny.

As they bet, Jonas raised with a blue chip for the first time. Dare. Both Sloan and Derek called. Janine glanced at her full house and decided to have a little fun. She tossed in a black chip. Ultimate Dare. It was time to shake things up a bit.

Everyone tossed in their black chips, then revealed their cards.

"I win," Janine said, then glanced toward Jonas.

It was time to warm things up with him. She had the feeling he was a little shy.

"Jonas." She smiled. "I dare you to join me in the closet for five minutes."

She stood up and started walking toward the hallway. Jonas leaped to his feet and followed her.

"Derek, can we use the closet in your bedroom?" She knew he had a very neat walk-in closet, so they wouldn't be tripping over shoes or knocking their heads against a shelf.

"By all means."

Derek stood up and followed them. So did Sloan.

She walked into the master bedroom, then opened the closet door and stepped inside. Jonas followed her in and closed the door. Neither of them turned on the light.

She reached out and found his hard chest, then stroked her hands over his shoulders. In the darkness, he drew her toward him. Her breasts brushed against hard muscle, then his arms wrapped around her and he pulled her tighter against him, driving her hard nipples into his solid chest. He groaned and spun them both around. His big, hard body pressed her against the wall and he kissed her, his mouth hard on hers as his tongue pushed past her lips. She sucked on it, welcoming it deep into her mouth.

Man, this guy was anything but shy.

His hand found her breast and he cupped it, squeezing as

his tongue plundered her mouth. Then he released her lips and kissed down her neck, then her chest, until he found her hardened nipple and captured it in his moist mouth. In the dark, with this virtual stranger touching her, suckling her nipple, she felt faint with need.

A loud knock startled her.

"It's been five minutes," Sloan called.

Oh, God. Leave it to Sloan to actually time us.

Jonas sucked one more time, then released her aching nipple. He moved away and the door opened. She drew in a deep breath and peered into the lighted bedroom, then followed Jonas out of the closet. Sloan's gaze fell to her breast and she glanced down, seeing her one nipple standing more at attention than the other, and a little darker in color.

At his frown, she simply smiled at him and continued into the dining room, then sat down.

The next hand went to Dare, with Derek the winner.

"Janine, I dare you to tease my cock with your mouth for five minutes."

She grinned. "I accept your dare."

He stood up and she walked around the table to him. She crouched down and reached into his boxers, then drew out his erection. She wrapped her hand around his veined member, then kissed the tip of him, totally conscious of Sloan's intense gaze on her. Swirling her tongue around and around, she teased Derek's cockhead, then glided downward, swallowing his big corona in her mouth. She sucked a little, then glided lower. Derek's fingers stroked through her long hair. Sucking again, she glided up, then released him. She licked him from base to tip, like a long, hard lollipop, then licked him again.

In her peripheral vision, she could see Jonas stroking his own cock through the cotton of his boxers. The knowledge she was turning on three men at once sent thrills through her. She wrapped her lips around Derek's erection and swallowed him, opening her throat so she could take him all the way to the base. He groaned in pleasure.

"Time," Sloan said, his voice tight.

She squeezed Derek inside her mouth. For a moment, she was sure he was going to come, but somehow he held back. She glided upward and released his marble-hard member. She smiled and stroked her finger the length of him, then tucked his erection back inside his boxers.

The next round also went to Dare. This time Jonas won.

"Janine, I want you to stroke yourself."

She stood up and ran her hands over her breasts, teasing the nipples.

"No, I meant . . . inside your panties," Jonas clarified.

Sloan's gut clenched at Jonas' words. It was bad enough he was watching with such eagerness as she caressed those gorgeous breasts of hers, but now he wanted too much.

"He didn't specify that—" Sloan started.

"Don't worry about it," Derek said, his gaze glued to her fingers as she tweaked her nipples.

Damn it. Rules were rules. But he bit back a protest as Janine glanced at him and their gazes locked.

"Sloan, it's just a friendly game," Janine said.

"Yeah, very friendly," Sloan muttered.

As Janine compressed her lips, he sucked in a breath. Damn

it, what the hell was he doing? He had to convince her he was all right with this kind of shenanigans. He wasn't getting off to a very good start.

"And friendly is great," Sloan added halfheartedly.

Janine nodded, then turned her gaze back to Jonas. She smiled warmly, which tore at Sloan's heart. He wanted her to smile at him that way. And *only* him.

One of her hands abandoned her breast and glided down her trim midriff. His breath caught as her fingers dipped under her panties, and he couldn't help imagining the feel of her silky curls. The black lace of her tiny panties moved as her fingers glided back and forth between her legs. Sloan stared in fascination, imagining what it would feel like to slide his own fingers down there. His cock throbbed with need. He dragged his gaze away and glanced toward the other two men. Clearly, they were both imagining the same thing.

"Time," Sloan said hoarsely.

He had no idea if five minutes had passed, or if the others would argue with him since no time limit had been set, but Janine stopped and no one argued. Seeing both other men with their hands on the huge bulges in their boxers, he figured they probably couldn't handle much more and still keep playing the game, either.

Janine sat down and all Sloan could think about was the fact that her pussy had to be really wet, making her panties damp. As if to confirm, she grabbed a tissue from the box on the table and wiped her fingers.

Derek dealt the next hand. Sloan couldn't help staring at Janine's naked breasts the whole time. Damn, it was hard to concentrate on his cards. When Janine won the hand with a green chip—clothing—he and the other two men gazed at one another, then stood up together.

Her gaze flickered back and forth across all of them as they tugged at their elastic waistbands.

"Okay, guys. I want to enjoy this. One at a time." She glanced toward Derek. "You first."

Derek slid his thumbs under the waistband of his boxers, then drew them down. His cock fell forward, hard and pointing straight at her. He sat down, but his cock still peered up through the glass tabletop.

"Nice." She turned to Jonas.

He tugged on his boxers, then drew them down slowly, revealing the tip of his penis, then slowly drawing the fabric down his long shaft. Finally, he dropped his boxers and they glided down his legs.

"Mmm. Impressive." She practically drooled as her gaze traveled up and down the length of Jonas' erection, which stood quite tall.

She turned to Sloan with a wicked grin. "Now you."

As Sloan pushed one side of his boxers down his hips, he tucked his hand against his rock-hard cock, holding it against his body, then pulled the other side down. He noted that Janine's gaze locked on the tip of his cock as it peeked above the fabric. She watched hungrily as he revealed more of his long shaft. He released his cock and it leaped forward as he pushed his boxers farther down and let them fall to the floor.

Her eyes widened as his full erection bobbed up and down.

Five

Janine couldn't believe it. She'd never seen a cock as big as
Sloan's before. She could just imagine it pushing into her,
stretching her like she'd never been stretched before. Her
insides ached with need. God, that cock could be inside her
right now if she just said the word. Should she drop the restriction banning sex between them tonight?

Damn, no. She'd made that decision for a good reason—
both for Sloan and for Jonas. Anyway, it wouldn't be fair
to Sloan for her to be on-again, off-again. Of course, he'd be
happy about it tonight—a guy would never pass up the opportunity for sex, even serious, play-by-the-rules Sloan—but
tomorrow . . .

He'd never take her seriously again.

Oh, God, the look of hunger in Janine's eyes as she stared at
his cock nearly sent Sloan off the deep end. He wanted her so
badly right now. He gritted his teeth under her feminine
scrutiny.

Derek handed her the deck and she shuffled and then dealt the cards. Her breasts bounced a little with her movements. Sloan's gaze never left Janine's hard, dusky rose nipples. Pushing forward so delightfully. He could imagine their pebbly texture in his mouth, the sweet taste of them against his tongue.

When he looked at his hand and saw he had a straight, he pushed the betting to Ultimate Dare, and won.

He stared at Janine with hunger. "I dare you to ten minutes in the bedroom with me."

"All right." She smiled casually as she stood up.

He grabbed her hand and dragged her into the bedroom. When they were face-to-face behind closed doors, she stared at him quizzically.

"What now?" she asked.

As his gaze lingered on her deliciously round breasts with the nipples straining forward, he realized he hadn't really thought this through.

"Well, I'd like to drag you into my arms and drive my cock deep inside you," he muttered, "but I promised I wouldn't. So I guess we just stand here for ten minutes."

She gazed at him with sympathetic blue eyes. "I know this is super hard on you, but I really think it's for the best."

He nodded, his teeth clenched.

"Look, how about we do a little something to put on a good show for the others. You do have your masculine reputation to protect." She stepped back from him, then stroked her hands over her breasts.

Heat washed through Sloan like a high fever.

"Janine, if you don't want me to jump your bones, you really should stop doing that."

She grinned. "Oh, I think you'll survive. I trust in your strength of will."

Elation shot through him at her words, followed by doubt as he watched her fingertips play over her hard nipples. Could the strength of will she so admired in him stand up to this kind of torture?

She continued to flick her fingertips over her tight buds and began to make whimpering sounds. Then came little murmurs of pleasure in her throat. Soon those murmurs turned to moans. His cock twitched in need. He could barely stop his hands from reaching for her and pulling her against him. He wanted so desperately to stroke those lovely breasts of hers, to feel them against his chest.

But she trusted him not to, and that trust gave him superhuman strength.

She moaned loudly, gasped, then moaned again. His cock throbbed with the need to be inside her as she continued to moan louder and louder, as if in the throes of passion.

"Oh, yes . . . oh, yes." She winked at him as she squeezed her nipples. "Sloan, I'm—" She gasped and threw her head back. "Oh, God. I'm coming." Then she wailed loudly.

God, he practically came on the spot.

She grinned widely and her gaze fell to his throbbing erection. She covered her mouth and giggled quietly. "Oh, my goodness. You can't go out there like that. Not now."

Damn, she was right. No guy would believe he hadn't just come if he'd been actually fucking her.

And, damn, he wanted to fuck her.

He pulled her against him and groaned at the sensations assaulting him. Her soft breasts pressing against his chest, each bead-hard nipple driving into him. Her warm belly compressing his throbbing cock between them.

His tongue drove into her as he wished his cock could, and her hot mouth surrounded his tongue. Heat spiked through him. Oh, God, he was going to—

Releasing her lips, he grasped her hips and pulled her tight against his body, then groaned. His body tensed and his cock erupted. His body shuddered as he climaxed, hot liquid spewing between them.

He cupped her head and held it tight to his chest, his fingers tangled in her long blond hair. God damn it, this wasn't the way he'd imagined his first time with her would be.

Would she think . . . ? Did this mean he'd failed her test?

"Janine, I didn't mean to." He sucked in air. "You aren't going to count that as . . . ?"

He hesitated when he heard a whimper against his chest. Damn it all. Had he made her cry?

"Janine?" As he tipped up her chin, he realized she wasn't crying. She was trying to muffle laughter.

"What the hell is so funny?"

"That was certainly one solution to our dilemma."

"Dilemma?"

"Well . . ." She pointed at his wilted cock. "It's not hard anymore."

"That's true." Damn. How did this woman manage to keep him so totally off balance all the time? "If we stay in here any longer, though, the same problem will . . . crop up . . . very quickly."

She glanced down at his already swelling cock. She grinned

and stroked her finger over the tip, nearly driving him to distraction. How could she touch him so casually and not realize the profound effect she had on him?

"In that case, I'd better give you some space." She backed away and grabbed a tissue box from the table beside the bed and wiped up the gooey mess from her stomach. She handed him several tissues, too.

"I'll just go clean up a little."

She headed for another door on the other side of the bed, probably an en suite bathroom, which reminded Sloan that she knew her way around Derek's bedroom. Jealousy surged through him, but he quashed it as he cleaned up the wetness on his stomach.

A knock sounded on the door.

"Hey, guys. If you've decided to abandon us, at least let us know so we can put on a movie or something," Derek said through the door.

Janine wandered back into the room, then headed toward the door. "We're coming out now, guys."

She glanced at Sloan. "You ready?" She glanced down at his cock, which was already halfway to full erection again. She grinned. "We'd better get out there before we have to start all over."

At the thought of a repeat performance, his fingers twitched with his desire to pull her into his arms again, but he sucked in a deep breath, then nodded.

"Let's go."

Sloan opened the door and strode from the room. The others followed him back into the dining room.

"Whose deal?" Sloan asked.

"Mine." Jonas grabbed the deck of cards.

Everyone slid their hands from the previous round toward Jonas and he swept them up and began shuffling.

"Now that we're naked"—Jonas glanced at Janine, his gaze dropping to her breasts—"at least most of us, how do we handle betting? I mean, if our highest bet is a green chip, we don't have any clothes to take off."

"Right." Derek stood up and grabbed four black chips from the case and brought them back to the table, then tossed one to Jonas and to Sloan and collected their green chips. "Instead of a green chip, you'll have to go straight to a blue one, then black. The extra black is in case the betting goes all the way up to four chips."

"So we might owe two Ultimate Dares?" Sloan took a sip of his beer.

"That's right." Derek pushed aside his own green chip.

"So when Janine bets a green chip, each of us bets a blue one." Jonas said as he dealt.

Derek nodded.

Jonas picked up his blue chip and rolled it between his fingers. "But even though we would owe a Dare, Janine would still have to strip. If she lost the hand."

"As long as her highest bet was a green chip," Derek answered.

Sloan's gaze shot to Janine's skimpy black lace panties, as did the other guys'. He picked up his cards. Two aces. He discarded three cards, then picked up the new ones to discover another ace and a four.

"Stay." As great as his hand was, he didn't want to raise to the next level because he hoped Janine would, then they would all call, forcing her to lose those sexy little panties of hers.

"Stay," said Derek.

"I'll stay, too." Janine grinned, clearly deciding to torture them.

Jonas narrowed his eyes as he gazed at her. "I'll call."

They all laid out their cards. Sloan's three aces won.

He stroked his chin as he stared at Janine. "Truth, hmm?"

There were many things he'd love to know about Janine that he was fairly certain she would avoid telling him, especially about her unusual sex life, but in the context of this game she probably would.

"How many men have you made love with at one time?" he asked.

She stared at her cards lying on the table. Was she going to avoid answering? Then she glanced up at him and smiled. "Three."

Even through jealousy surged through Sloan at the thought of three men manhandling Janine, his cock throbbed with need.

Jonas raised an eyebrow. "Really? Three at once?" His cock twitched.

Derek simply smiled, but the veins on his cock seemed to pulsate. Sloan wondered if Derek had been one of the three.

Sloan tossed his red chip to the center of the table, followed by everyone else, then shuffled the cards and dealt. Sloan had two jacks. Everyone discarded and Sloan dealt replacement cards, then glanced at Derek.

"I stay," Derek said.

Janine studied her cards, then pursed her lips in a tiny smile. "Stay."

"I raise," Jonas said, tossing in his blue chip.

Sloan picked up his three new cards. Four jacks. Damn,

as much as he'd like to see her remove those panties, he'd really love to get some mileage out of such a great hand.

"I raise." Sloan glanced at Janine and smiled, then tossed in his blue chip and one of his black ones.

"Stay," Derek said, adding his two chips to the pot.

Janine gazed over her cards, considering. He watched her fingers trail over the chips, then flick them up and down. Had he scared her off? Finally she picked up her green and blue chips and pushed them forward. "Stay."

"Me too." Jonas added his blue and black chip.

"You didn't want to raise, Jonas?" Derek asked.

"Are you kidding? I'm not going to win with this hand"— he turned over his cards to reveal five random cards—"and I'd rather chance that the action stay out here where I can see it."

Right now, Janine's highest wager was a Dare, and it was her wager that defined what would happen, since she would either win or be the one chosen by the winner for the Dare. If Jonas had pushed it to an Ultimate Dare, whoever won would take her somewhere private.

"Good point." Sloan flipped over his cards, showing his four jacks.

"Beats me." Derek showed a pair of threes.

They all stared at Janine.

She pursed her lips. "Aw, gee." She flipped over a hand with three fives. "That beats mine, too."

Sloan wanted to prove to her that he could cope with her being with other men in front of him. Since she still had her panties on, there was at least a barrier in place, however small. So he'd choose something with both men. But first, he wanted to warm her up. A little payback for what she'd done to him in the bedroom.

"First, stand up."

She stood.

"Now I want you to slide your hand inside your panties." His cock ached as her hand slid under the black lace. "Now push your fingers inside yourself and stroke, then glide back to stroke your clit. Keep doing that, back and forth, until you're almost ready to come." He smiled. "Then stop."

She grinned. "Okay."

The lace moved as her fingers glided inside the crotch of her panties. Her cheeks became flushed and her breathing accelerated.

"How does that feel, Janine?" he asked.

She nodded. "Good." Her voice was breathless.

Her fingers moved faster. Jonas' hand wrapped around his cock and he stroked. Derek's hand found his own cock. Sloan kept his hands steadfastly away from his erection.

Janine rapidly sucked in air, her fingers moving in rapid pulsing movements within her panties. Then she gasped and froze, her face flushed. She sucked in several deep breaths, calming herself. She sat down.

"No, don't sit yet."

Her eyebrows quirked.

"I have a dare for Derek and Jonas, which involves you."

"But I thought we'd agreed that the winner would choose one player to do the Dare," she said.

"Well, technically, we said the winner could choose which player performed the action, but we didn't say they were limited to only one."

"I'm okay with it being more than one," Jonas said.

"As am I." Derek stood up.

"I bow to the majority." She stood up and placed her hand on her chest under her naked breasts, then performed a small bow.

"Good. Now, Derek stand in front of Janine."

Derek walked forward and faced her.

"Jonas, stand behind her," Sloan instructed.

Jonas walked behind her.

"Move in closer." He watched as the men shifted closer to her. "I want you to close in tight. Show her what it feels like to be sandwiched tight between your bodies."

Six

Janine could hardly catch her breath as the men moved in closer. She'd come so close when she'd stroked herself she had almost lost it. Now Derek's big, solid chest pressed against her breasts, and his erection pushed against her stomach. Jonas moved closer. His body pressed tight to her back, his big cock pushing against her ass. Oh, man, the room felt like a sauna.

"Guys, show her a little taste of what you'd like to do to her."

Jonas' hands slid around her body and cupped her breasts. Derek stroked over her hips, then down into her panties. Keeping one hand firmly on her breast and toying with her nipple, Jonas glided his other hand down and dipped into her panties, too. His fingers glided over her wet slit right alongside Derek's.

"Oh, God, she's so wet." Jonas glided a finger inside her and she melted between him.

"Guys—" She sucked in a breath at the intoxicating pleasure rushing through her. "If you both keep—" She gasped. "Oh, God . . ."

She moaned as pleasure swamped her senses, catapulting her over the edge. Derek flicked her clit as his lips found her neck and nuzzled. Jonas pumped his fingers inside her and she clenched around them, which intensified her pleasure. She gasped and cried out.

The men continued to stroke her as she rode the ecstasy to its culmination. She collapsed back against Jonas. He wrapped his arm around her waist, his other hand still cupping her breast, and held her tight to his body, his cock still hard and twitching against her ass. Derek smiled down at her, then kissed her lightly on the lips as his hand slid from her panties.

Finally, the men eased away from her. She walked to her chair and sat down, glad to give her wobbly knees a rest. She glanced at Sloan but couldn't tell anything of his mood from his poker face. She'd hate to play poker with him if she actually cared about losing.

She threw her ante in along with the others and Derek dealt out the cards. She glanced at hers. A pair of queens and three low cards. Knowing she'd kept the men waiting long enough, she tossed aside the queens, and asked for two more cards. Her new hand was a total loser.

She smiled. "I raise." She tossed in her green chip.

All the men smiled, then a quick repetition of the word *stay* resounded around the table, along with the clinking of chips adding to the pot. Everyone revealed their cards, all the men grinning happily. Derek won this time. Not that it mattered. Their gazes all turned to her.

Excitement quivered through her as she stood up. First, she ran her hands over her breasts, then she flicked her nipples. Need fluttered through her. She tucked her thumbs under the waistband of her thong, then glided one side down her hip slowly, totally aware of every heated male gaze watching her. Then the other side. She pushed a little farther, until her curls barely peeked over the top.

She paused, smiling at their intense expressions. Swaying her hips from side to side, she turned her back to them. She pushed her panties down her thighs, leaning forward as she glided them down her legs, giving the men an eyeful of her naked behind. She pushed the tiny panties to the floor and stepped out of them, leaving her legs parted slightly, then slid her hands up her inner thighs as she slowly stood up again.

When she turned around, every male gaze locked on her groin.

"Damn, but that's a thing of beauty!" Jonas' hand was wrapped firmly around his cock, squeezing as if it would burst.

She smiled broadly, pleased she'd decided to trim the curls on her mound into the shape of a star and shave the rest of her sex bare.

She sat down, purposely not crossing her legs. All the men continued to stare at her through the glass tabletop, sending heat flooding through her.

Her gaze landed on Sloan's enormous cock and she imagined it pushing inside her, the big, bulbous tip caressing her insides. Her vagina clenched in need. Damn, she'd had no idea what he'd been hiding in those jeans of his.

"I think it's time we toss aside the red chips and ante with blue," Derek suggested.

"Good idea," said Sloan.

"Let's do it." Jonas still gripped his erection.

Janine's gaze slid to Jonas' fingers, and she watched them glide over his long shaft. Sloan's big cock was off-limits—tonight—but Jonas' looked mighty fine right now.

Derek scooped away the red chips in the pot, along with Janine's green one and pushed them to the side, then glanced to her. "Okay, Janine?"

She dragged her gaze from Jonas. "Okay."

She tossed in her blue chip as ante along with the others, then fumbled through a quick shuffle of the cards and quickly dealt.

All she had was a mishmash of cards, but three were spades so she threw away the other two. To her surprise she drew two more spades. No one raised. Clearly everyone had decided, as had she, that staying in the room on a Dare was the most exciting prospect right now.

Her flush beat everyone else, so she smiled and stood up, picked up her shawl from the back of the chair, and laid it on the table. Then she sat on it, spreading her legs wide.

"Jonas, I dare you to come over here and tease me with your mouth."

He leaped to his feet and stood in front of her, gazing at her curls hungrily.

"Where?"

She opened her legs wider and said in a sultry voice, "Anywhere you want."

Sloan and Derek moved around to stand behind Jonas, all of them staring at her fuzzy star. Jonas stepped closer and ran his hand along her shoulder, then leaned forward. His lips caressed her neck, sending tingles down her spine. She rested her hands on his warm shoulders. Such broad, strong shoulders.

He kissed downward to her breast, and then his tongue curled over her nipple. Hot and wet. She tightened her hands on his naked flesh. He licked, then opened his mouth and the tip of her breast disappeared inside. His tongue continued to stroke her tight bud, and he sucked lightly. She sighed and her gaze locked on Sloan. He watched her face intently. Again, she could not decipher his expression.

Sloan watched as Jonas did things Sloan had always dreamed of doing to Janine. Nuzzling her neck. Tasting those lovely rosy nipples. Kissing downward to her more intimate places.

Jonas stroked his finger over one point of the golden star-shaped patch of curls on her pussy. Sloan resisted wrapping his hand around his aching cock and stroking it. God, he wanted to touch her there, to slide his fingers inside her.

Jonas sat down on the chair in front of her, then wrapped his hands around her calves and lifted them until her feet perched on his knees, which he spread wide, opening her to their view. Jonas leaned forward and nuzzled the star with his nose.

Sloan's cock throbbed with aching desire. Jonas glided down and his mouth covered her naked folds. Janine sucked in a deep breath. Jonas must be licking her. Maybe gliding his tongue into her. His hands stroked her inner thighs. She opened even more, then gasped, her fingers forking through his hair.

Sloan could just imagine his own tongue dabbing against her clit, then licking it. He would suck the tiny button while he slid his fingers inside her, then find her G-spot and stroke until—

She gasped and moaned, clearly approaching orgasm, but Jonas leaned back and grinned at her, his lips glistening. Wide-eyed, she stared at him.

"I wouldn't want you too complacent right now," Jonas said.

He stood up and Derek slapped him on the back, chuckling. She pushed herself off the table and stood up, not even noticing when her shawl slipped to the floor. Sloan grabbed it and hung it over her chair again.

"Um . . ." She glanced around, then grabbed the deck of cards, not even gathering the discarded hands from the last round. "Instead of a full hand, why don't we just draw. High card wins."

She took a card then plunked the deck on the table. Jonas and Derek each took a card, and Sloan grabbed the next one. A king.

"How about we stay with the current stakes," Sloan suggested.

"That's fine." She laid her card on the table. "I've got a ten."

Sloan revealed his king of hearts.

"Beats me," said Derek, flicking aside a seven of diamonds.

"Me too." Jonas tossed his five of clubs on top of the other cards.

Sloan gazed at Janine. "Well, now. You're such a daring young lady." He rubbed his chin. "I think you can handle a very daring challenge."

She gazed at him, eyes bright in anticipation, clearly ready for more. He was ready, too. Unfortunately, he couldn't be the one to give it to her. But he damned well wouldn't mind watching the other men give her pleasure right now.

"I dare you to give Derek a lap dance, and make both Derek and Jonas come at the same time."

The other men smiled broadly.

Janine's heart pounded in her chest as she stood up and grabbed Derek's hand. Her body blazed with need as she led him to the leather couch in the living room. Smiling at her, he sat down and she climbed onto his lap, facing him, her knees on either side of his legs. She pushed herself right up and arched forward, her breasts an inch from his face. He wrapped his big hands around them, lifting them higher, then brought one to his mouth and lapped at the nipple.

She dropped her head back and moaned softly. He licked the other nipple, then took it in his mouth and sucked. She arched her pelvis forward, rubbing her hot opening against his hard, ridged abdominal muscles. She glided downward until her hot flesh bumped against his hard erection. She pushed it against his stomach with her hand, then lowered herself onto his thighs. She rolled her pelvis forward, pushing her wet flesh against his hard shaft, then rolled back and forward again. He grasped her ass and tugged her tight against him, then guided her hips in circular movements on him.

She drew away and stood up, repositioning herself on her knees over his lap, but with her back to him. Both Jonas and Sloan sat across from them, watching. She smiled and wrapped her hand around Derek's erection, then lowered herself until her melting flesh brushed it. She stroked his member forward and back, the tip brushing against her slick flesh. Derek murmured approving sounds. Jonas and Sloan stared intently at where she caressed herself with Derek's cockhead. Then she lowered herself onto Derek's marble-hard member. Slowly. His hard flesh stroked her vagina as she moved. Down. Until he filled her completely.

Derek's hands cupped her breasts. He lifted them, his thumbs stroking over her nipples. Jonas wrapped his hand around his straining cock. Sloan's fingers curled tightly over the armrests of his chair. His cock stood straight up, an impressive length. Janine licked her lips as she thought about licking him, then taking him inside her mouth.

She rolled her hips in a circle. Derek's cock swirled inside her and her eyelids fell closed at the intense pleasure. She ran her hand over her belly, then glided downward to where she was joined with Derek. Her finger found her clit and she stroked it. She fell back against Derek's solid chest as he caressed her breasts and she flicked her clit.

She smiled at Jonas and curled her finger in a come-hither gesture.

He stood up and walked toward them. As soon as he stood in front of her, she leaned forward and wrapped her hand around his cock. Full and solid. Curved a little to the right. She tucked her other hand under his balls and caressed them in her palm.

"Oh, yeah." Jonas ran his hand along her cheek, then through her hair.

Derek released her breasts and glided his hands over her belly as she leaned forward and wrapped her lips around Jonas. He moaned as she swallowed his cock, her tongue swirling over the tip.

She rolled her hips on Derek, his cock caressing her insides as she glided down on Jonas, taking his shaft deep into her mouth. Jonas ran his hands through her hair at her murmured sounds of pleasure. His big cock in her mouth. Derek's big cock in her vagina. Heat thrummed through her.

She glided off the end of Jonas' cock and gazed at his face. "Your cock is so good in my mouth. With both your cocks inside me, I could come right now." She smiled. "But I won't until both of you come."

His hazel eyes darkened. She sucked him back into her mouth again.

Derek found her clit and stroked it lightly. Pleasure rocked through her body. Jonas found her breasts and cupped them, then squeezed. She squeezed his cock in her mouth, then sucked. Derek grasped her hips and his cock shifted inside her as he pivoted her hips in a rocking motion. She cupped Jonas' balls and dove down on him, taking him as deep as she could, then drew back slowly, squeezing and sucking him hard. His balls tightened in her hand and she knew he was close.

Her hips pivoted faster. The stroking of Derek's cock inside her sent pleasure rocketing through her. She pumped her mouth on Jonas faster, then felt his body tense. She squeezed Derek's cock inside her and he moaned. Hot liquid erupted into her mouth as Jonas grunted. Derek stiffened beneath her and groaned loudly. She grabbed Jonas' spent cock as it slipped from her mouth and stroked him as she continued to ride Derek's cock. Derek flicked her clit and wild, rapturous sensations pulsed through her, and she wailed in an explosion of ecstasy.

Finally, she collapsed forward and wrapped her arm around Jonas' waist and leaned against him, her cheek resting against his hard, ridged stomach. He stroked her hair gently. Derek caressed her back.

Finally, Jonas crouched down and faced her, cupped her cheeks and kissed her. Then he took her hands and helped her to her feet.

"I went ahead and drew cards for all of us for the next round," Sloan said.

Janine glanced toward him. She'd actually forgotten he was there.

"As it turns out, you won." He smiled broadly. "What will your dare be?"

She glanced around at Derek, still sitting on the couch, and Jonas. She smiled at Jonas.

"I dare you to take me into the bedroom and fuck me like crazy."

Jonas grinned. "What we just did was crazy, but"—he grabbed her hand and led her toward the bedroom—"I'm game."

Seven

Janine followed Jonas, moving at just short of a trot to keep up with his long strides. As they reached the bed, he spun around and took her in his arms. His mouth captured hers, then his tongue plunged into her mouth and drilled deep. She could feel his wilted cock rising between them.

He released her mouth and lifted her onto the bed, then climbed on right after her. As he prowled over her body, she noticed Derek and Sloan standing across the room. They'd followed them into the bedroom.

Jonas glanced over his shoulder. "Are you guys staying?"

"It was a Dare, not an Ultimate Dare."

That meant no privacy. Not that she needed it, but Jonas might.

His hard cock brushed against her belly. Well, that quelled any concerns she had of performance anxiety because of an audience.

He kissed her neck, then drifted lower and captured her hard nipple in his mouth. He squeezed, then sucked. She moaned at the delightful sensations. He pressed his knees between her thighs and she opened for him. His hand found her wet slit and he stroked, three fingers gliding inside her. She squeezed them, already hot and ready for his big cock.

Her gaze drifted to Sloan, who now sat on a chair off to the right, near the end of the bed. Her gaze lingered on his enormous cock and she wondered what it would feel like to have that exceptional erection inside her.

Jonas' thumb found her clit and she sucked in a breath. He shifted upward and captured her mouth again. He positioned his cockhead at her opening and pressed it into her. His corona filled her. He glided deeper, his shaft caressing her inner passage. Deeper, until his body pressed tight against her.

He kissed her again, then began to move. His cock stroked her as he pulled back, then drove deep again. She clutched his shoulders as he thrust again and again, driving into her faster and faster, until her body quivered with pleasure. She couldn't help imagining what it would feel like to have Sloan fucking her right now, his big cock stretching her.

"Do you like that?" Jonas asked.

"Oh, yeah." She clung to him as he pulsed faster inside her.

He thrust deeper, pinning her to the bed, then drew back and thrust again. Pleasure vibrated through every cell in her body.

He drove in again. "Are you going to come?"

She nodded, unable to find the breath to speak. With his next thrust, she moaned, then catapulted into ecstasy. He kept pumping into her, driving her pleasure higher, then groaned his release.

Sloan could barely stand it. His jaw clenched. He'd barely contained himself enough to stop from pulling the guy off her.

It was one thing to watch her with the two guys fucking and sucking in the living room on a couch, but watching Jonas fucking her on the bed, making her come in soft, murmuring sighs . . . It was way too intimate for his liking. *He* wanted to be in bed with her like that. *Inside* her like that. Driving her to ecstasy. With his name on her lips.

He would definitely find a way to make that happen.

Very soon.

Janine stepped into the night air with Sloan, Derek, and Jonas behind her. She almost hated for the evening to be over, but spending the night with all three men, especially with her restriction on Sloan, wouldn't work out very well. They walked to Jonas' car.

Jonas unlocked the car and pulled open the front passenger door for Janine.

"You said your sister lives out in Maple Grove," Sloan said to Jonas. "Since my place is just a few blocks from here, why don't you drop Janine and me at my house, then I'll drive her home from there," Sloan suggested. "That way you don't have to go out of your way."

Jonas glanced to her. "Is that okay with you?"

She hesitated. She didn't want to inconvenience anyone, and there was no reason she shouldn't be alone with Sloan. It might be a little awkward between them after the night's events, but it would be a good opportunity to find out what he thought about the evening—good or bad.

If he didn't think he could handle continuing this type of relationship with her, it would be good to talk about it now.

"Okay. Sure."

Derek glanced at her and their gazes met. She smiled and nodded, knowing that if she'd shown any sign of not wanting to go with Sloan, Derek would have stepped in.

She was sure Sloan didn't miss the exchange.

"Well, good night, Janine." Derek drew her into his arms and kissed her soundly, his tongue dipping into her mouth briefly.

She got in the car and Jonas closed the door. Sloan climbed in the seat behind her. Jonas started driving, and Sloan directed him until they pulled in front of a lovely brick house with a sporty-looking red car with sleek lines and a sunroof sitting in the driveway.

Sloan got out of Jonas' car, and opened the door for Janine.

"Thanks, Janine." Jonas stood in front of her, seeming a bit uncertain.

She stepped forward and grasped his shoulders, then tipped her head up for a kiss. His arms wrapped around her and he brushed his mouth on hers. She slid her tongue between his lips and coaxed him into her mouth, then sucked lightly on the tip of his tongue.

She eased back and smiled at him.

"Thank you for a wonderful evening, Jonas."

He beamed back at her. "Anytime."

He glanced to Sloan and nodded, then got into his car and drove away.

She stepped toward Sloan's car.

"Very nice." She'd never pictured Sloan driving a sexy, sleek car like that. "What is it?"

"It's a 2002 Pontiac Firebird." He unlocked the passenger door and opened it for her.

She ran her fingers over the glossy red finish, then got inside and sank into the contoured leather seat.

Sloan closed the door, then climbed into the driver's seat. The engine roared to life, and moments later they were speeding along the highway.

"So what did you think of tonight?" Janine asked.

He glanced her way, then back to the road. "You want to talk about it here?"

She shrugged. "Not if you don't want to."

"Why don't we talk about it at your place?"

At her place? Was he going to ask to come up?

Probably. Well, why not? She just didn't want him to pressure her to have sex with him.

He took the off-ramp from the highway.

But why would he? He had expressly agreed to no sex with her tonight. Of course, it was after midnight and Mr. By-the-book Sloan might feel that meant the limit was off. Plus, he had been kept in a constant state of arousal tonight, with no relief.

Her gaze fell to his crotch, and even in the darkness she could see a hint of the huge bulge she'd noticed in his jeans after they'd dressed before leaving Derek's apartment.

He pulled into the parking lot for her apartment building and parked in a visitor spot. He got out of the car, then opened her door and walked with her to the front door.

He followed her inside, then summoned the elevator. As

they rode up together, she wondered if she should discourage him from coming in.

Once at her door, she turned the key in the lock, then glanced to Sloan.

He raised an eyebrow. "Are you going to ask me in or do I kiss the bejesus out of you in the hallway where all your neighbors can see?"

The thought of his body pressed against her, his mouth assaulting hers, triggered a hormonal rush. She opened the door and stepped inside. "Come on in."

She kicked off her shoes as he closed the door behind him. His hands came around her waist and she found herself pressed against him, staring into his cobalt blue eyes. He captured her lips and she melted against him. As his tongue explored her mouth, excitement skittered through her. All she could think about was his body, so solid and muscular. His arms so firm and strong around her.

His cock so hard against her.

She stepped back. It wasn't fair to lead him on like this. She wouldn't let it go where he wanted it to go. Not tonight.

"Janine, I want to be close to you. Let me stay the night."

She hesitated. "Sloan, we agreed we wouldn't—"

"I don't mean to have sex. A deal's a deal. I just want to hold you."

She gazed at him, her eyebrows quirking. "Do you really think you can do that?"

He grasped her shoulders, his gaze locked on hers. "I'll do whatever it takes to be with you."

He dragged her against him for another kiss. His tongue drove into her, coaxing her tongue into a tumultuous dance, weakening her resolve. He sucked her tongue into his mouth.

Heat washed through her as his breathing became erratic. She needed air.

She pressed her hands flat on his chest and eased back.

"If you keep that up," she said breathlessly, "we'll have a repeat performance of earlier."

Except that with his rock-hard cock pressing against her, and her imagination churning with images of what it would feel like for that huge member to glide inside her, filling her like no man had ever before, she feared it might be she who came on the spot.

Her joke didn't soften the burning question in his eyes.

"Let me stay, Janine."

She toyed with her ring. "Sloan, it would be a lot easier if—"

"I don't care about easy. I care about being with you. You know you can trust me to keep my word."

She sucked in a breath, knowing that he spoke the truth. She could trust Sloan with her life. And she could certainly trust him to keep his word—even when the promise was not to fall prey to his own built-up desire. He'd already proven that several times tonight.

"You certainly are persistent."

His lips turned up in a smile. "That's one of my charms."

"All right. I give in."

He drew her close again, his arms draped loosely around her waist. "That's what I want to hear. You submitting to my will." He nuzzled her temple.

She pulled back as she said, "I'm not submitting—"

But he tugged her against him again, ending her words with a kiss. He stroked her long hair back and gazed down at her. "Too bad. You might want to try it sometime."

She sucked in air, not even wanting to think about what it would be like to submit to Sloan's dominating authority. Finally just to give in and let him take control.

She trembled at the thought.

"I . . . uh . . . why don't I make some coffee?"

"Why? Do you want to stay up all night?" His grin sent her off balance.

"Of course not. I meant decaf."

He stroked her hair behind her ears, sending her insides quivering at the tender intimacy. Her heart thundered at the thought that soon they'd be in bed together. Because she knew that's what he intended when he asked to spend the night. Though why he'd do that to himself, knowing they would not be having sex, she didn't understand.

Not that she'd find it easy. Knowing she just had to say the word to experience the ride of her life on that enormous erection of his.

"Where's the bedroom?" he asked.

Sloan followed Janine down the hall, wondering why the hell he was willing to put himself through this. But as his gaze glided along the gentle curve of her waist, then lingered on the sway of her hips, he knew exactly why.

He just wanted to feel her body against his again, to hold her in his arms.

He wanted the intimacy of spending the night with her, just the two of them.

If that meant a night of sheer torture, with a rock-hard cock and no relief in sight, so be it. It would be worth every agonizing moment.

Janine slipped off her dress and turned her back to him as she shed her bra, then pulled on an oversized T-shirt. She climbed into bed. Sloan stripped off everything but his boxers, then lay down behind her. He drew her soft body close to his. As his cock pressed against her, he thought he'd die from need.

"You seem pretty interested in more than sleep," she said.

"I'm fine. A promise is a promise."

"So you're just going to tough it out?"

He wrapped his arm tighter around her waist. "I wouldn't exactly call this a punishment." He nuzzled his lips against the back of her neck. "As far as agonizing tortures go, this is pretty sensational."

She laughed, then wiggled her behind against him.

"Well, you are a cruel and heartless woman, aren't you?"

She turned in his arms, her face bright with her smile, but when their gazes locked, her smile faded. Her focus dropped to his lips and he couldn't help himself. He leaned forward and captured her soft, luscious mouth. His cock grew harder, wanting to be inside her.

He drew back. What the hell was he doing? He wouldn't last two minutes this way, let alone a whole night.

"How about you turn around now?" he suggested.

Janine pursed her lips, then rolled away. What the hell was she doing? She wasn't trying to encourage him. She wasn't even sure why she'd allowed him to come in. He said he'd stick with her rule that the two of them not make love tonight, but she didn't know if he'd make it the whole night, not with the way he'd been teased all evening, watching the others with her. He must be turning blue by now.

She didn't want to be mean to him, but she couldn't just let go of her rule now. If she did, he wouldn't take her seriously. He'd always been such a strong, overwhelming presence in her life. When she'd moved to Kenora, she'd finally come into her own, found herself—and gotten comfortable with who she was. She needed him to realize that and to respect it. It was the only way any kind of relationship between them was possible.

Yet that kiss had knocked her totally off balance. Sweet and meltingly hot. Reaching into her heart and squeezing, leaving her breathless. Damn, but she wanted to kiss him again. To turn back into his arms, press her body tight to his, and surrender her lips to his masculine mouth. Let him explore, first her mouth, then her breasts, then . . . Her insides quivered and she clenched her vagina as it burned with need. Oh, God, she wanted him.

She held still, trying to relax despite his warm breath teasing the back of her neck. His strong arms curled around her waist. His erection pressed against her backside. God, he was huge. This was going to be a long night.

Eight

Sloan opened his eyes to sunlight, intensely aware of his painfully hard cock and Janine's soft behind pressed snugly against it. The night had been long and nearly unbearable with the intense need pulsing through him. He'd barely slept a wink.

But he wouldn't have given it up for anything.

He tightened his arm around her waist.

"Good morning." Her voice sounded sleep-softened and sultry.

He flattened one hand on her stomach. Sometime during the night, her T-shirt had ridden up over her hip. He glided his other hand along the curve of her hip, exulting in the feel of her silky, naked flesh.

Janine could feel his massive cock pressed against her, still as hard as a rock. How had he lasted the whole night like that? And, just as promised, he'd never made a move on her.

She turned in his arms.

The feel of her breasts gliding against his chest at her movement, only a thin layer of cotton between his naked body and hers, sent his cock twitching.

He gazed at her, taking in her angelic beauty. Mussed blond hair in wisps around her face and half-open eyes simply added to the soft, ethereal quality.

He tipped up her chin and brushed her lips with his. A quiver went through him at the effect of her soft mouth moving under his. He deepened the kiss, gliding the tip of his tongue between her lips. Her tongue brushed against his, sending his pulse rocketing. Her breasts crushed against him, her mouth moving under his, sent a powerful need cascading through him.

Oh, God, he wanted her.

Janine melted against Sloan as his tongue gently explored her mouth. Her hard nipples pressed into him and she wanted him to touch them, to tease them. His mouth moved away from hers and he nuzzled the base of her neck, sending a frenzy of need quivering through her body. He kissed across her collarbone, but she ached for him to move downward to her needy breasts.

Last night's promise was fulfilled, and today was a whole new day.

He eased back and gazed at her face. She rolled onto her back and tugged her T-shirt over her head. He smiled and his gaze glided to her breasts, warming them with the heat of his desire. She wanted him to cup them, to take her hard nipples into his mouth. She arched her chest upward.

"You have beautiful breasts." His gaze lingered on them, switching from one to the other. But he didn't touch them.

Was he waiting for an invitation?

Suddenly she realized that's exactly what he was waiting for.

Her fingers curled around the side of the sheet. Would she let him get away with that? Force her to ask for what he should just do naturally in this situation?

But she remembered how he'd held back last night, totally resisting his obvious desire for her. He'd done everything he could to follow her rules. The least she could do was humor him with this.

"Sloan, do you want to touch them?"

He smiled. "Yes, I do." But he made no move to do so.

Okay, he was going to be like that.

She smiled coyly. "Sloan, please touch my breasts."

"My pleasure."

He stroked her shoulders, then down her chest. When his big, masculine hands covered her breasts, the heat surrounding her, she sucked in a deep breath. He stroked and squeezed her gently, sending need pulsing through her. She wanted his mouth on her, sucking her nipple deep into his mouth.

"Oh, Sloan. That feels so good."

His fingers stroked over her distended nipples, and then he captured one between his finger and thumb and squeezed lightly. She gasped at the intense sensation.

"Please, take it in your mouth."

His cobalt blue eyes darkened and he leaned forward and covered her hard nipple with his lips. She moaned softly at the feel of his hot man-mouth surrounding her. She stroked her fingers through his dark, wavy hair as his tongue toyed with her bead-hard nipple, stroking it and gliding over the aureola. Then he sucked her deep into his mouth and she gasped, holding his head tight to her breast.

He drew back and captured her other nipple, teasing it relentlessly, then sucking deep. She gasped again, her insides aching with need.

He eased back and gazed down at her, a half smile on his lips.

How could he just stare at her like that? Wasn't he going insane with need himself? He'd been hard all night long.

She reached for his immense cock and wrapped her hand around him. It was rock-hard and so thick she could barely wrap her fingers around it. She stroked him several times. His eyes closed and she could tell he used a great deal of will-power to hold back. She sat up and dipped toward him to take him in her mouth, but he grasped her shoulder, stopping her.

"Not a good idea right now."

She nodded and lay back down. Heat thrummed through her as she stripped off her panties, then arched her pelvis. She wanted him to drive that big cock right into her. His gaze glided downward and rested on her trimmed curls.

But he did nothing.

"Sloan, I want you."

His half smile broadened. "Tell me what you want."

"I want you to fuck me."

His smile faded. "I'm not going to fuck you, Janine."

Confusion swirled through her. "You aren't?"

"No." He glided his hands along her thighs, opening them.

He knelt between her legs and brushed his fingers over her curls. Then he stroked along her damp slit.

The sensation of his fingers touching her there sent thrilling sparks through her. She widened her legs and he pressed his huge cockhead to her opening.

"I'm going to make love to you."

He pushed forward and his cock slid in a little, then he drew back. He pushed a little deeper, then drew back again. The third time he pushed in deeper still, until his whole cockhead filled her. She sucked in a deep breath, getting used to his huge girth inside her. He caressed her breasts, stoking her building arousal. Then he began moving forward again. Slowly. Stretching her. She gasped as he pushed deeper than any man had ever gone before.

She clung to him, holding him tight to her body.

"Oh, God, Sloan. That feels so good."

He chuckled, then drew back, denying her his solid shaft. Then he drove forward again.

"Oh, my God. Yes."

He filled her and she thought she'd burst on the spot. He drew back and thrust forward again.

Pleasure spiraled through her in a dizzying cacophony of sensations.

"Sloan. Oh, yes."

He pulsed forward again and she moaned.

Sloan watched her face as it blossomed in total bliss.

"Sloan, I'm—" She gasped and clung to his shoulders. "Oh, God, I'm coming."

He almost lost it on the spot, but with sheer willpower he held off his own desperate, aching need to erupt inside her as he thrust into her again and again. She wailed and clung to his shoulders as she shot off to ecstasy.

She calmed and gazed up at him uncertainly, her face still glowing with pleasure. He thrust again and erupted inside her with such force it was amazing he didn't rocket straight to the ceiling.

She held him tight to her body as he continued to pulse and twitch inside her.

"My God, I could feel that. I've never actually felt a man come inside me. That was amazing."

He grinned at her, then kissed her soundly. The kiss turned to passion and he pulled her tight against him, then rolled them both to their sides. Her lips moved under his and their tongues tangled. Finally, he released her mouth and simply held her tight in his embrace.

After a few moments, she shifted a little.

"Um, you know you're still inside me, right?"

Was she kidding? How could he *not* know?

"Yup." He kissed her forehead, then closed his eyes.

"You planning on going to sleep like this?" she asked.

He opened his eyes. "That had been my plan."

Her lips pursed. "And if I have other plans?"

He flattened his hand on the small of her back and pulled her tight against him. She gasped as his semierect cock glided deeper.

"Do you?"

She gazed at him with glazed eyes. "Do I what?"

"Have other plans?"

"Oh, uh . . . No, not really."

He grinned broadly, loving the fact he'd been able to throw *her* off balance for a change.

She gazed at his chest as she stroked her hand down it, then squeezed internal muscles designed to confound a man, gripping his cock in deliriously intense, warm woman-softness.

"I'm just not sure I want to . . . sleep," she said.

"I'm pretty tired after last night."

She pushed against his chest. He cooperated and rolled onto his back, taking her with him.

"How about I do all the work?" She settled her knees on either side of him and sat up. He ran his hands over her gorgeous breasts, then cupped them, the soft mounds filling his hands.

"Honey, if you think this is work, I'd love to see what you consider pleasure."

She laughed, stroking her fingers over his tight nipples, sending spiraling swirls of heat through him.

He couldn't believe he'd finally made love with Janine. It had been his dream for so long.

And now, here she was wanting more.

She leaned forward and kissed his neck, then nibbled his raspy chin.

She shifted her hips. The tight grasp of her silken sheath sent his cock twitching.

"Ohhh, yeah." She sighed. "Sloan, you have one serious piece of equipment there."

"You like?"

"I *love* it!" She swirled her hips around one way, then the other, spiraling his cock inside her.

"Baby, that is sensational." He grasped her hips and followed the movement of her body as she drove him wild.

She squeezed and twirled. His cock swelled close to bursting. He stroked down her belly and tucked his finger at the base of her, then explored her folds until he found her clit. She sucked in a breath as he toyed with it.

She began to move with more purpose. She pulsed against him, pivoting her hips forward and back. He flicked faster against her clit and she moaned. Her head fell back, her long blond hair cascading behind her.

"Oh, yes. Oh, Sloan."

Oh, God, the sound of his name on her lips at the height of passion . . .

She moaned, and he felt his groin tighten. He burst inside her again.

"Sloan. Yes. I'm—" She wailed as she joined him in ecstasy.

She dropped down onto his chest, her soft breasts snuggling against him. He wrapped his arms around her waist and breathed in the heavenly herbal scent of her hair.

Then his eyes fell closed and consciousness slipped away.

Janine snuggled her cheek against Sloan's broad chest, stroking the solid muscles. She couldn't stop smiling. Sloan was full of surprises. His huge cock was one. Wowee! But his playfulness was also unexpected. And the way he'd handled last night. Sure, he'd had a few tense moments, a little jealously showing through, but given how much she'd pushed him, he'd done amazingly well. Almost too well. She'd expected him to fail miserably, proving to him that he couldn't handle dating her. She'd never expected to get to this point with him.

A low rumbling snore startled her. Her eyes widened. The man had fallen asleep?

She lifted her head and stared at him, ready to whap him one. But as she gazed at his handsome, endearing face, relaxed in sleep, she remembered how he had held her all night long, his cock as stiff as a board. He couldn't have gotten much sleep.

She sighed and sat up, easing away from the warmth and comfort of his broad chest. As she pushed herself onto her knees, his big cock slid from inside her. She sighed at the feeling of emptiness it left.

She walked to the bathroom to shower. She had to be careful she didn't get too used to Sloan and that addictive cock of his—and, if she were honest with herself, the wonderful feeling of being protected and loved in his arms—because as far as Sloan seemed to have come, she was certain that he would not accept her lifestyle in the long run. Knowing him as she did, she realized he probably hoped to insinuate himself into her life, and her heart, then start insisting on changes she wouldn't want to make.

And that she couldn't allow.

Sloan awoke and immediately missed the softness of Janine's body next to his, the feel of his cock nestled deep inside her warmth.

He opened his eyes to bright sunshine flooding through the bedroom window. Janine's bedroom.

He glanced at the clock. Damn, eleven thirty. He'd wasted the whole morning sleeping instead of spending the time with Janine. Having a leisurely breakfast. Talking. Getting closer to her. He tossed aside the covers and headed into the bathroom to shower. When he walked into the living room fifteen minutes later, dressed and clean-shaven, his hair still damp, Janine glanced up from the dining table, turning over the magazine she'd been reading.

"Morning. There's fresh coffee in the kitchen." She stood up and stretched. "I'll make you some breakfast. You still like western omelets?"

He grinned. Janine making him breakfast? Delightful.

"I do."

"Okay, coming right up."

He followed her into the kitchen and poured himself a coffee, then watched as she beat eggs in a metal bowl. She walked across the kitchen and pulled a container from the fridge with the ham, peppers and green onions already chopped.

"Aren't you efficient."

"I made one for myself a few hours ago, so I cut up extra. I figured you'd like one when you got up."

He dragged his hand through his damp hair. "Yeah, sorry about falling back to sleep."

She grinned. "Well, you did expend a lot of energy this morning." She glanced down at his crotch, causing his cock to swell. "And after almost no sleep last night."

He wanted to sweep her into his arms again and carry her back to bed, but she turned away and opened the lower cupboard by the oven. She pulled out a frying pan and put it on the stove, turned on the element, then added butter to the pan. Once it was melted, she poured the egg mixture into the pan and added the other ingredients. After a few moments, she turned the omelet.

"Smells good." Sloan grabbed a plate from another cupboard and retrieved some cutlery from the drawer.

Janine lifted the steaming omelet onto his plate, then sat across the table from him sipping coffee and reading through her magazine while he ate. He couldn't take his eyes off her, wanting to memorize everything about her. Her long hair cascading over her shoulders, the sunlight glistening from the pale golden strands. Her teeth nibbling on her sweet, full lips, just as he'd love to do right now. Her glossy burgundy polished fingernails catching the light as she flipped the pages to find another article to read.

This was heaven, simply spending time with her . . . like any couple might do. It was so rare that Janine did anything like anyone else. He admired her uniqueness. Her no-fear attitude to fly in the face of—well, pretty much anything—to just be who she was. But it was exhausting. In some things, he wished she could just be like everyone else. Like when it came to love and relationships.

"So how's your job going?" he asked.

She glanced up from the colorful pages. "Good, actually."

"You still work at The Fitness Place, right?"

She closed the magazine and pushed it aside. "That's right." She sipped her coffee.

"Clearly you make good use of the equipment because you look fabulous."

"Thanks, but I don't work in the gym anymore."

In L.A., she'd worked as a fitness trainer while she'd gone to college, then took a job as manager after she graduated.

He'd thought she'd had greater career aspirations after studying kinesiology and business, but she seemed to enjoy the work, and that was the important thing.

"So what do you do now?"

"I moved here to take a job as regional manager. There were a couple of locations that had openings, but I chose here because it's close to headquarters and that means more opportunities for career advancement." She leaned forward and gazed at him. "Don't you remember me telling you that? And how excited I was?"

His chest compressed. He remembered her bubbling about her new job and the new town she'd be moving to, but the details of her job had blurred at the emotional punch to his gut.

"I remember how excited you were, but all I heard was that you were leaving."

Nine

The pain in Sloan's compelling blue eyes tore at Janine's heart. All thoughts of her job and hurt that he hadn't really taken an interest in her new career melted away.

His fingers wrapped tightly around his mug. "My life was so empty after you left. I was a total idiot for not realizing I was driving you away."

Her heart ached at his strained voice.

She shook her head. "No, you didn't, I just . . . I needed to be on my own."

Sure, going to Kenora offered career advancement, but there were other jobs she could have pursued in L.A.

She drew in a deep breath. "I needed to get away from the memories of Ben."

Sometimes the pain had been unbearable. She didn't want to forget Ben, but she also didn't want constant reminders of her devastating loss.

Sloan nodded, Janine's pain reflected in his eyes. She knew how much he missed Ben, too.

"And you needed to get away from me."

"It was a good career move," she insisted.

He nodded. "I know. More opportunities for career advancement." He took her hand. "You don't have to protect my feelings. I realized after it was too late that I'd been smothering you. I was overprotective and overbearing."

She squeezed his hand. "You meant well."

She couldn't believe she was downplaying what had been such a huge deal to her for such a long time, but seeing his vulnerability, having him open up to her like this, threw her off balance. She didn't want to hurt him.

She'd never wanted to hurt him.

He had only done what he'd done because he cared about her.

"Sloan, why did you come to Kenora?"

She'd thought it odd he would show up here of all places, and she didn't want to believe he'd come here because of her, but that was the only thing that made sense. And deep inside, it warmed her heart while at the same time it terrified her.

"I needed a change, too," he said. "I figured if you loved living in Kenora, it must be a great place to be."

So there it was. Confirmed. He had come here specifically to pursue her. Her heart clenched. Damn it. How could she deal with that? Him uprooting his whole life and coming here for her? She didn't need that kind of pressure.

She glanced at his empty plate. "Are you done?"

"I guess I am. It was delicious."

He rose and placed his mug and plate in the dishwasher. She followed him to the sink and rinsed her own cup, then handed it to him. He put it on the rack and closed the door.

Then he gazed at her and smiled. He placed his hands on her shoulders and drew her toward him, then captured her lips. She swore to herself, knowing she should have stepped away before he could lay his hands on her again. When he did that, she lost all reason. And when he kissed her . . .

His tongue swept into her mouth and a tidal wave of hormones swelled through her. Her arms encircled his neck and she moved her lips with his, swept away in the passion.

He drew back and gazed down at her, his intense blue eyes searing through her.

"This morning was incredible." He brushed his lips against her temple, sending tingles dancing down her spine. "I've dreamed of being with you like that for so long." He nuzzled her neck. "It was everything I'd hoped for. And more."

His hands stroked down her back, then cupped her behind and pulled her against his body. An incredible bulge pressed against her pelvis, and her insides quivered as she imagined that big cock of his gliding into her again.

But more than that, her heart melted at the thought of him stroking her with his big masculine hands. Feeling the tenderness of his touch as he explored her body, as his lips and mouth aroused her in sweet and loving ways.

His hands glided away, then found the buttons of her blouse. He unfastened one, then the next. Anxiety warred with excitement. She stilled his hands.

"I . . . uh . . . sorry, Sloan, but . . . I have plans. I really have to get going."

"Can't you cancel?" He sent her a devilish grin. "I'll make it worth your while."

She had no doubt about that, but she did not want to

mislead him by giving him the idea that they could settle into a relationship with just the two of them. It wouldn't be fair to him.

She drew away. "No, I'm afraid not."

Disappointment glazed his features, but he released her. Feeling like a total bitch, she walked toward the doorway. "I have to go get ready."

"Can I give you a lift somewhere?"

She glanced back at him from the doorway. "No, that's okay. Thanks." Then she hurried to the bedroom, wondering if he'd still be there once she'd finished changing.

As Sloan stood at the door, he drew Janine into his arms and kissed her again, not wanting to leave, but she drew herself from his embrace and stepped back.

"So what are your plans this afternoon?" she asked.

"Well, a buddy is moving this weekend and I told him I'd help him unload the truck. He should be ready in a few hours."

"That's great. Maybe I can meet him sometime."

He didn't know whether to take that as a hopeful sign that she thought it might work out between them—and she would start meeting his friends—or if she meant that she'd like to add his friend to her harem of men.

"Maybe. I'm more interested in when I can see you again."

"Well, I can set up something for next Saturday, if that works for you. Jonas won't be in town, but Derek could probably join us."

He raised an eyebrow. "That's not what I had in mind."

"Oh? And what did you have in mind?"

He smiled and stroked her cheek. "Just the two of us would be nice."

She sighed and gazed at him like one might a child. "Sloan, I told you right up front that I'm not interested in an exclusive relationship."

"One date doesn't mean we're exclusive."

"But you're not talking about one date, are you? You'd like every date to be just the two of us."

"That's pretty normal for most people, you know."

"Yes, but not for me. And not with you. Not when you're trying to prove that you can handle my dating style."

He compressed his lips. He had hoped that after last night and this morning, she would realize that her attraction for him could be so much more . . . that she could fall in love with him . . . and then she would *want* to be alone with him.

Of course, maybe his plan *had* worked. Maybe she had realized exactly that and now wanted to put distance between them because she didn't want to give up her wild lifestyle.

Either way, his best shot seemed to be to show her he could be just as wild as she could.

"All right, then. I have a proposal."

She quirked her head. "I'm listening."

"Derek arranged a stranger fantasy for you, but my appearance ruined it."

She grinned. "Well, as things turned out, I wouldn't exactly say it was ruined, since it's led to such an interesting turn of events."

He smiled. "Good. But I still feel I owe you one. How about I set up a stranger fantasy for you?"

Her eyebrows arched upward. "You?"

"Sure. Why not? I have friends."

She pursed her lips and gazed at him. "Okay. Bring it on."

Sloan grabbed the last box, labeled KITCHEN, from the rental truck and carried it into Liam's new house.

"Any more?" Liam asked as Sloan placed the box on the pile in the corner of the kitchen.

"Nope. All done." Sloan grabbed a cola from the fridge and pulled open the tab, then took a sip. Moving was hot work.

"I've ordered pizza. We can take a break and then get to the unpacking."

Sloan grinned. "What if I told you I have a hot date and can't stay for the unpacking?"

"I'd say I don't believe you, because I *know* you wouldn't leave me with all this unpacking. Especially after Derek bailed on me."

When Sloan first moved to Kenora, he and Liam had hit it off immediately. They'd wound up on a weeklong training course together out of town and spent time after hours bonding over beers. At the time, Liam had been going through a rough time in his long-term relationship. He'd needed a friend to talk to, and Sloan had been happy to listen. Sloan had rediscovered how good it could be to have a good buddy to share with, something he hadn't had since Ben's death. He'd even told Liam about Ben, touching on his heartache with Ben's sister but without giving too much away, and definitely without revealing that Janine lived in Kenora now and that he planned to pursue her. He wasn't ready to reveal that much of himself to anyone.

After they got back from the course, Liam tried to improve things with his girlfriend but eventually figured out that it was never going to work and broke it off, which led to his moving into the new house.

The doorbell rang and Liam strode down the hall to answer it. He returned a few moments later with a pizza box.

"Talking about hot dates . . ." Liam opened the pizza box and pulled out a slice, then dropped it onto a paper plate and handed it to Sloan.

"I was just kidding. I'm not going anywhere. I'll stay until every box is unpacked."

"I was thinking more of last night. I called your place last night, then again his morning, just to confirm when you were coming over, and I couldn't get you."

"Oh, I'll give you my new cell number."

"Sure, but . . . are you seeing someone?"

Sloan shrugged. "There is a woman I've been seeing. Nothing serious."

He wasn't about to admit he had deep feelings for Janine, not even to Liam. If things didn't work out . . . if he failed to win her over . . . Damn, it was none of anyone's business.

Liam watched Sloan's face. Something was going on in that thick head of his. Not something he'd share. Sloan didn't tend to share. Stuff, sure. And his time. But nothing about what went on in that head of his.

Except that time they were on the training course together. After Liam had spilled his guts about his own relationship problems, Sloan had actually revealed something of himself. And it explained why Sloan was generally pretty guarded. It wasn't hard to figure out it had a lot to do with the friend he'd lost years ago, a cop who'd died in the line of duty. Sloan had even told Liam that was the reason he'd had joined the police force.

There was something about the friend's sister that still haunted Sloan. Not that he'd said too much about it, but he'd said enough for Liam to figure out Sloan had been head over heels for the woman. In fact, Liam might be too much of a romantic, but his gut told him she was *the one* as far as Sloan was concerned. But he'd lost her, and clearly that tore him up inside.

Whatever it was, Liam would do anything to help him sort it out. Sloan deserved some happiness, and the way Liam saw it, he'd never find it if he didn't learn to loosen up.

Sloan put his paper plate on the counter and leaned back. "Listen, talking about women . . ."

"Women? I'm all ears, buddy. I'm a single man now. And just so you know, I'm beyond ready to start sowing my wild oats again."

"Yeah, well, that's what I wanted to talk to you about. There is this new woman I'm seeing."

Sloan hesitated. Maybe he was going to open up after all.

"The one who's nothing serious," Liam said.

"That's right. I have . . . kind of a strange request."

Liam sipped his root beer and waited, giving Sloan time to figure out what he needed to say.

"This woman . . . she's into some wild and crazy things. She likes a lot of excitement."

Liam raised an eyebrow. "You want to borrow my motorcycle?"

Sloan glanced at him, interest in his eyes. "That's not a bad idea, but it's not what I was going to ask."

"What, then?"

"She's into . . . more than one man at a time."

Liam laughed. "You're kidding." This must be some kind of joke. That was not Sloan's type of scene. Derek's maybe— no, definitely. But Sloan?

"I'm dead serious. I promised to set her up with a special fantasy. Sex with a stranger. Are you willing to help me out?"

"And I'd be the stranger?"

"She knows me, so . . . yeah."

"And you and I"—he flicked his finger back and forth— "would both . . . ? At the same time?"

"That's right. You in?"

Liam's groin tightened at the thought. If this hot babe was as wild as Sloan claimed, how far would she go to please a guy? What would she let a guy do to her?

"Are you kidding me? When and where?"

Janine entered Sloan's house and glanced around. It suited him, with the strong, robust lines of the furniture, the dark colors, the nature art on the walls.

"A glass of red wine?" Sloan asked.

"A vodka cooler would be nice."

She sat down on the burgundy leather couch as he headed into the kitchen, then returned a moment later with a tall glass of clear, bubbly liquid. She sipped the drink, then set it down. Her glance landed on the two stripper poles in the corner of the room about two feet apart. They were those pressure ones, so they could be dismounted easily.

"I take it those are for our little adventure tonight."

He sat beside her. "True. I understand you have a penchant for handcuffs." His hand stroked along her shoulder, left bare by her halter-style dress.

She smiled. "Are you going to use handcuffs on me?"

He kissed the side of her neck, sending tingles quivering through her. "Well, I wouldn't want you to peek at your stranger. And I wouldn't want you to run away."

"Run away? Because the stranger will ravage me?"

He nuzzled the sensitive flesh at the base of her neck and heat washed through her. "Ravage you. Yes."

He tucked his finger under her chin and turned her face, then captured her lips. His arms encircled her and he pulled her against his solid body.

A chirping sound interrupted them and he drew away, then pulled his cell phone from his pocket and glanced at the display.

"My friend is almost here. It's time to get you ready."

She picked up her glass and took a couple more sips, excitement zinging through her. "Okay. Let's do it."

She stood up and walked toward the poles. Sloan grabbed a pair of handcuffs sitting on the end table beside the couch and clamped one bracelet around her wrist. He backed her up to the poles and fastened her to one of them. Then he fastened another cuff around her other wrist and fastened it to the other pole. His stared straight down, his gaze lingering on her breasts swelling from her plunging neckline.

"Mmm. Nice view." He picked up a black satin eye mask and positioned it over her eyes. A thin elastic strap held it in place. "Can you see anything?"

She shook her head. "Not a thing." Total blackness filled her world.

She felt his warm hands on her shoulders and tingles danced through her as they glided down her arms.

"My friend will be here in a few moments." He stroked over her breasts, then cupped them. "I left the door unlocked. He'll walk in any moment."

Sloan leaned close. She felt his breath on her ear, then felt the soft brush of his lips.

"He'll see me touching you." His fingers slipped under her halter dress and inside the cup of her strapless bra. "He'll see me caressing you."

He teased her hardening nipple with his fingertip. "Then he'll touch you, too. And caress you."

Heat washed through her.

Had she heard the door open? Was there someone else here?

Sloan's fingers glided down her back . . . then she realized he was undoing the zipper of her dress. He untied the halter strap at the back of her neck and the dress dropped to the floor. She felt naked and exposed, even though she still had on a bra and panties. A strapless black lace bra and a tiny thong held up with a rhinestone waistband. She felt sexy and wanton—and vulnerable.

And intensely turned-on.

Sloan's lips found hers, and he kissed her soundly.

"My friend's here," he murmured.

Ten

Janine felt Sloan slip away.

Silence filled the black void around her. It would be easy to believe that she stood in a dark room where the men could not see her. But their world was full of light, and they—*he,* this stranger—could see her perfectly well, standing there wearing barely anything at all.

She could feel the stranger moving close to her. His heat, or an energy about him, or something. Then she could feel his breath on her temple as he leaned close to her.

"You have a safe word?"

His voice was deep and a little gravelly. *Very* sexy.

"Yes," she answered.

"Tell me what it is."

"Dragon."

"Good."

Something touched her shoulder and she almost jumped. He stroked lightly across her shoulder, then down her arm. Goose bumps quivered along her skin.

"Say your safe word again."

"Dragon."

He brushed his raspy cheek against hers and murmured, "Now don't say it again unless you mean it. If you say the word 'dragon' I will end this immediately. Understand?"

She nodded. Excitement quivered through her at his air of complete authority.

"I can't hear you."

"Yes, I understand."

"Good. Now, you are doing this of your own free will, right? It was your idea?"

"Well, originally, it was my idea, but Sloan—"

"Just answer the question." He stroked a finger along her cheek. "You agreed to have Sloan bring me here—a stranger— to have sex with you?"

"Yes."

"Good." He stroked along the side of her neck. "Because I want to have sex with you. You are a very beautiful woman. Very sexy." He stroked downward, then brushed his finger-tips over the swell of her breast, above the lace edging of her bra. "I'd like to see your naked breasts, so I'm going to take off your bra." His fingers continued along the other cup. "I'm not asking your permission. I'm just doing it."

His hands glided around her, the heat of him enveloping her, and he released the hooks of her bra. She felt the fabric peel away from her body. As soon as the cool air hit her skin, her nipples hardened.

"Your breasts are quite lovely."

She felt the light touch of something brushing her nipple, and it tightened even more.

"And I see you're turned-on."

She felt his face close to hers.

"I'm turned-on, too," he murmured in that sexy, gravelly voice.

His lips nuzzled below her ear, and she almost cried out as tingles raced down her neck and through her aching body.

He cupped her naked breasts, enveloping them in the warmth of his big hands. He kneaded them as he nuzzled her neck, then kissed downward. She gasped as he caught one nipple in his mouth. He licked it, then swirled his tongue over it. She arched against him, his mouth on one breast, his hand on the other, still caressing her. He captured her other nipple, sucking it gently at first, then with more intensity.

Finally, he drew away. She could feel his hot gaze on her.

"You look so hot standing there, your breasts naked, your nipples standing up, hard and needy. If I asked you to, would you touch yourself?"

She pulled at the chains holding her hands away from her.

"If I free your hand, would you touch your pussy? Stroke it for me?"

"Yes."

He grasped her right wrist, and she heard a click and the metal bracelet around her wrist unfastened. He lifted her hand and pressed his lips to her palm. He kissed it, then ran the tip of his tongue along her skin, tracing a line on her palm. Her insides fluttered and heat seeped through her. He pressed her hand to her belly, then downward. She felt his finger tuck under the elastic of her thong and draw it forward. Then he guided her hand underneath the fabric.

He released her wrist and she stroked her fingertips over her curls.

"Tell me what you feel."

"I feel the hair."

"You aren't shaved?" he asked.

"I've trimmed it. Into a star shape."

He chuckled. "I can hardly wait to see."

She pushed her hand deeper into her panties, her finger-tips stroking her slit.

"Are you stroking your pussy now?"

"Yes." She stroked over it several times, the flesh becoming more damp.

"Is it wet?"

"Yes."

"Push your fingers inside."

She slid her fingers into the slick heat of her vagina.

"How wet are you?"

"*Very* wet."

"I can hardly wait to feel how wet you are. Now push your fingers in and out."

She did as he said, getting hotter with each stroke. He cupped her breasts and caressed them, his thumbs toying with her nipples. Then his hands glided down her body and he tugged at the elastic of her thong.

"I want to see your fingers pushing in and out." He pulled down the front of her panties, exposing her fingers.

She pushed inside again. He drew her panties down her thighs, to her ankles.

"You have a beautiful pussy."

His finger traced the star as she continued to glide in and out of her slick folds.

"My cock is hard from watching you. Do you want to touch it?"

"Yes, please."

He grasped her wrist and guided her hand forward. Her fingers came in contact with hot, hard flesh. She wrapped her slick fingers around a solid shaft.

"You are wet. I can feel the wetness on your fingers."

She stroked his big shaft, gliding to the tip, then cupped her hand around his cockhead, teasing under the ridge with her fingertips. He twitched. She glided down again and felt his testicles against her fingers. She slid underneath and cradled them in her hand, caressing them.

"I want you to suck my cock," he murmured in a hoarse voice. "Would you do that for me?"

"I'd like that."

"I have a stool." Sloan's voice startled her.

She'd forgotten he was still here, watching them.

Sloan's hands grasped her hips from behind. "I've put it behind you. Just sit down."

He guided her as she sat down. She felt the cushioned surface beneath her, then settled onto it. Sloan's hands slid up her body, then stroked her hair back from her face.

The man in front of her released her breasts and Sloan's hands cupped them in his place. She wrapped her hand around the big cock in front of her and drew it to her lips. She licked his shaft, then lapped her tongue over his tip.

"Your mouth feels good on me."

Encouraged, she wrapped her lips around his cockhead then she took him into her mouth. She tightened around him and swirled her tongue over his tip again. Around and around. Then she slid forward, taking more of his shaft, solid, hard, its veins pulsing.

She pulled back and glided deep again. Opening her throat, she took him as deep as she could, satisfied by his groan of pleasure. His fingers stroked through her long hair as she moved up and down on him. She drew back, then swirled her hand around his exposed shaft while she sucked on his corona.

"Oh, man, that is heaven." But he tightened his fingers in her hair and coiled it around his hand, then drew her face away from his cock. "Now I want to watch you suck Sloan's cock."

Sloan released her breasts and a moment later, the stranger took her hand from his cock and guided it away, then pressed it to Sloan's cock. She wrapped her hand around it. Sloan stepped closer and she took the tip her mouth. As she swirled her tongue around his big cockhead, the stranger stroked her hair.

"His cock is so big I'm surprised you can get your mouth around it."

She glided downward, taking Sloan deeper. His big cock was a challenge, but she opened and took him deep into her.

"Impressive. Stroke the rest of his cock with your hand."

She swirled her hand around the thick shaft below her lips, then drew back, sucking him.

"Now both of us," Sloan said.

As she glided her lips from Sloan's erection, she felt another brush her lips. She felt for the other cock. Both cock-heads were touching side by side. She wrapped her fingers around the stranger's, then ran her tongue over one, then the other. She wrapped her lips around the stranger, and sucked, then released him and sucked Sloan's bigger head. One, then the other, back and forth. The stranger's slipped away and she licked the length of Sloan's long shaft.

"God, that's sexy," the stranger said. "Now suck him deep, and keep sucking until he comes in your mouth."

The sexy words sent electric thrills through her. She tightened her hand around Sloan's thick shaft, then pulsed up and down on his cock, squeezing him in her mouth. Her hands glided under his balls and she caressed while bobbing up and down.

"Oh, sweetheart." Sloan's hand cupped her head as she sucked and squeezed him.

His balls tightened in her hand, and he erupted in her mouth with a groan. She continued to squeeze him in her mouth until he stroked her cheek, then drew away.

"I'd like a closer look at that little star of yours," said the stranger.

She felt the stranger's hands on her knees, and he drew them apart as he knelt in front of her. He grasped her hips and eased her forward on the stool until she perched on the edge. She felt his fingertip trace the outline of the star shape as he had earlier. Then she felt his breath on her stomach . . . and the tip of his tongue grazing the top edge of the star.

He moved lower. His fingers stroked along the sides of her folds and she felt his tongue dip into her then drag along her wet slit. Then he covered her, his hot mouth enveloping her. His tongue teased her clit. His fingers found her wetness and glided inside her.

She grabbed his shoulder. "Oh, that feels so good."

He pulsed his fingers inside her and she tightened around him, but his fingers weren't enough. She wanted his cock. Then he sucked on her clit and bursts of light bounced around inside her head as pleasure spiked.

He sucked again and she moaned, an orgasm washing over her. His tongue continued to swirl over her sensitive nub, prolonging the pleasure.

Finally, he drew away and she gasped for air.

"Oh, please, fuck me."

"I told you she's a dirty girl," Sloan said. He took her free hand and clamped the handcuff around it again. "Stand up."

"Who do you want to fuck you, Janine?" the stranger asked.

"Oh, God. Both of you."

The stranger chuckled. "You're right. She's a very dirty girl." He wrapped his hands around her waist and pulled her close to his body. He was naked and his erection pressed against her stomach. "Do you want us at the same time?"

The thought of both cocks driving into her sent hormones coiling through her.

"Yes."

Sloan stepped behind her and pressed his body the length of hers, pushing her tighter against the man in front of her. Sloan was naked, too. Her breasts crushed against the stranger's chest, Sloan's huge cock pressed against her behind—she could barely catch her breath.

Sloan shifted his cock until it glided between her thighs and brushed over her slick slit. His cockhead pushed out in front of her and then he moved back and forth, stroking her sensitive, aroused flesh. The stranger stroked her breasts, then sucked one into his mouth. She moaned.

"Fuck me," she insisted.

Sloan's cock drew back, then brushed against her back opening. She stiffened and he chuckled.

"I think we'd better change positions," Sloan said.

The heat of their bodies moved away and then she felt their hard bodies sandwich her again. A big cock pressed between her thighs from the front. Sloan. He pushed his cockhead to her slick opening, then glided slowly inside. She whimpered at the intense pleasure of his generous girth stretching her. He went deeper and deeper, until she thought she couldn't take any more. Then he stopped, fully immersed in her.

He stroked his hands over her ass, then glided along her thighs, lifting her off the ground. She wrapped her legs around him.

"My turn."

She felt the stranger's cock press against her backside, pushing between her cheeks. His hard flesh felt slick. Lubricant. He pushed against her opening until she stretched around him. His cockhead pressed forward, sliding into her. He stopped for a moment, then eased forward again slowly, filling her. Finally he was fully immersed.

Both men's bodies pressed tight against her, their big cocks fully inside her. She felt so full.

Sloan drew back, then eased forward again. The stranger glided back and moved forward, following the same rhythm as Sloan. She sucked in air as the two hard males stroked her insides with pleasure, their cocks filling her again and again. She gasped as pleasure swept through her, clamoring through every cell in her body until she exploded in ecstasy. The men groaned. She felt Sloan erupt inside her.

Finally the men collapsed against her and held her between their hard bodies. After a few moments, the stranger moved away and she felt the cuff release on one of her wrists, then the other. She wrapped her arms around Sloan, her head resting on his shoulder. She reached for the blindfold, but he stopped her hand.

"Not yet." He scooped her up in his arms and carried her. A few moments later, she felt a bed beneath her as he laid her down. She felt the bed compress as he sat beside her.

"I want to watch while my friend fucks you," Sloan said.

"He'll need a little encouragement, though." He ran his hand over her nipple, and she got the idea.

She touched her nipples, brushing her fingertips over them lightly. "I liked your big cock in my ass," she said, undulating her body as she cupped her breasts and squeezed. "Now I really want to feel it inside me again." She slid a hand down her stomach to her slit, then pushed two fingers inside. "Here."

She felt the other side of the bed compress, then felt the stranger's hands on her breasts. He stroked them, then slid his hand down her stomach and over her slit. As she drew her hand away, he caught her wrist, then pressed his palm to the back of her hand and pushed a finger in beside hers.

"Let's do it together." He slid a second finger inside her, his other fingers and thumb wrapping around her hand. He guided her hand, moving their fingers in and out of her in unison.

Heat built in her rapidly.

She felt him brush her clit with his other hand, triggering a burst of wild sensations. Someone's mouth covered her breast and she gasped.

"I'm going to fuck you now," the stranger said as his fingers slipped away.

"Yes." Oh, God, she wanted him to.

He moved over her and she felt hard flesh push against her opening. His cockhead glided inside. She wrapped her hands around his shoulders. Broad. And muscular. She was sure he must be a cop, too. His cock kept pushing deeper, filling her. When he stopped, his groin tight against hers, his lips brushed her cheek, and he tipped up her chin and kissed her. The sweet tenderness of his lips against hers touched her. His tongue glided into her mouth and she moaned, then slid her tongue the length of his.

Then he began to move his body. Drawing back, then gliding deep again. Stroking her slick passage. She squeezed him, loving the feel of his cock inside her.

His gentle strokes became more insistent. His speed increased. His thrusts drove deeper. Wrapping her legs around him, she allowed him to go deeper still, then moaned as he filled her again and again.

"Oh, God, yes." Pleasure filled her. Pummeled her. Sent her shooting off the edge of sanity as she wailed in ecstatic bliss.

He groaned and lurched forward, his body shuddering with his release.

Finally, she dropped back on the bed, exhausted. She felt Sloan slide into bed behind her, sliding his arm around her waist, his body tight to hers. She fell asleep with the stranger still inside her.

Janine awoke to total darkness, with two hard bodies pressed against her. A pressure on her eyes made her realize she still wore the blindfold. She hooked her finger under the fabric and pulled the blindfold up. She blinked at the full sunlight filling the room, then stared at the face in front of her on the pillow.

The face of a total stranger.

His eyes opened and he smiled. "Good morning."

Eleven

Janine blinked. "Uh . . . yeah. Hi."

He stared at her with lively olive green eyes dancing with golden specks. His full, masculine lips turned up in a warm smile, and a few disheveled spikes of sandy brown hair lay across his forehead.

Oh, man, this was so strange. She'd never woken up to a total stranger in bed. The fantasy had been great, but she hadn't anticipated coming face-to-face with him in the morning.

Last night, when she'd almost pulled off the blindfold, Sloan had stopped her. But she'd been ready then, with her hormones still in high gear. Now, in the light of day, it just seemed . . . strange.

Then she felt his cock stir against her belly. In full arousal.

Sloan shifted behind her. His hands cupped her breasts and his cock—also hard—glided between her thighs, stroking her intimate flesh. At the feel of his warm, strong hands on her breasts, her nipples peaked, and memories of last night, with both men inside her, crept into her mind. As Sloan's hard flesh stroked over her slit, moisture pooled inside her.

Sloan stroked one hand down her stomach and positioned his cockhead against her opening, then pushed inside her. She sighed at the feel of his hard-as-rock cock sliding into her. He pulled the covers away, exposing her naked body to the stranger. Sloan grasped her hips and glided his cock in and out of her.

"Janine, meet Liam." Sloan glided inside her again. "Liam, meet Janine."

Sloan's big cock filled her again and again. His finger found her clit and she moaned at the intense sensations.

"Janine, take Liam's cock in your hand and stroke it."

She reached for the stranger's—Liam's—cock and wrapped her hand around it. She stroked as Sloan glided in and out in an easy yet maddeningly erotic rhythm. She squeezed Liam in her hand. He stroked her breasts, then teased her sensitive nipples. The wild sensations from their attentions collided into a building pleasure. She squeezed Sloan's cock inside her and arched against Liam's hands.

Sloan's cock glided deep inside her again, then back. And out.

She groaned at the emptiness. She squeezed Liam's cock and stroked more quickly, arching her body toward him. His compelling gaze captured hers and his warm smile melted her insides. He moved forward and pressed his cockhead to her opening. She lifted her leg onto his thigh and arched forward. His shaft pushed into her.

She clung to his shoulders, staring into his wonderfully handsome face and squeezed him inside her.

"Honey, that feels incredible." He drove deep, drew back, then drove deep again.

She curled her leg around his thigh, pulling him tight to her body. He thrust and thrust and pleasure shuddered through her. She clutched his muscular shoulders as his body speared into her, driving her to absolute ecstasy, her composure splintering as she wailed in bliss. Finally, he groaned and followed her to orgasm.

She rested her forehead against his chest and sighed. He might be a stranger, but she felt close to him. Maybe it was because of their sexual adventures last night . . . or maybe it was something more.

Liam kissed the top of her head, then shifted away as Sloan drew her onto her back, nuzzled her neck, and prowled over her. Janine gazed into Sloan's intense blue eyes, her heart thundering as his big cock pressed into her, then drove deep. She sucked in a breath as he pinned her to the bed, his cock filling her like no other. He drew back and began to thrust. She sucked in air, then moaned as an orgasm crashed around her. Building as he thrust and thrust. He erupted into her, catapulting her to blissful abandon.

He collapsed on top of her, then rolled to his side, taking her with him. Her head rested snugly against Sloan's solid chest as she caught her breath. Again.

"How about you two relax while I go make us some breakfast." Liam smiled as he pushed himself from the bed and padded away.

Janine stepped out of the shower and towel-dried her hair, then dressed. By the time she reached the kitchen, she could smell freshly brewed coffee and bacon.

"Anything I can do to help?" Her gaze lingered on Liam's tight, well-defined abs. All he wore were his dark gray boxers.

"Nope. Just sit and relax. I've got everything under control."

She sat at the table across from Sloan. Liam placed a plate of bacon and pancakes in front of her, then another in front of Sloan, and one at the empty place beside her. He poured some coffee into a mug and handed it to her, then sat down.

"So, Liam, how do you and Sloan know each other?" she asked.

"We were both sent on training just after he moved here. I was going through a bad time in a stagnating relationship and Sloan offered some good advice." Liam poured a little cream in his coffee and a spoonful of sugar, then stirred. He tapped his spoon on the side of the mug. "We've been friends ever since."

"So this difficult relationship . . . I assume it came to an end?"

"Yeah, we split a few weeks later. I stayed with my brother and his wife for a couple of months until I could find a place. I finally got into a new house last weekend."

She smiled. "You must be the friend Sloan went to help move last Sunday."

"Guilty."

"Well, you'll do fine out there." She winked at him. "The woman who ends up with you is going to be pretty lucky."

"Thanks." Liam took a sip of his coffee. "Right now I'm just trying to adjust to single life. I've lost touch with my old group of friends. The hardest part about being single is how much empty space I have to fill. So last night was really great for me." He sent her a devilish smile. "I must say, I can't re-member the last time I had such an enjoyable diversion."

Heat washed through her at the memories of him touching her body, her eyes covered by the blindfold.

"Me too," she murmured.

Sloan shifted in his chair and Janine glanced his way. His glower told her he was uncomfortable with her and Liam's mutual appreciation.

She turned her gaze back to Liam and grinned. "You know, Sloan's still fairly new to Kenora. I was planning to show him around town. You're more than welcome to join us if you'd like."

Liam grinned. "That would be great."

Boy, she loved his schoolboy grin. So charming. She wanted to run her fingers through his hair and tousle it.

Sloan, who'd been sipping his coffee, set down his mug. "Don't you still have a lot of unpacking to do?"

"No. You and I got most of it done last Sunday. Those few boxes that were left I organized the next day." Liam glanced at Sloan. "But if I'm intruding . . ."

"No, not at all," she said.

Janine took a bite of bacon, gazing innocently at Sloan's glare. Clearly, he'd hoped to ditch Liam this morning and have her all to himself.

"We could go to the zoo. Then maybe to Viewpoint Lake. There's a really pretty beach there with a view of the hills."

"Sounds good to me." Liam poured maple syrup on his pancakes. "Especially if I get to see you in a bikini."

Sloan stood up and took his plate to the counter, glowering the whole time.

A soft breeze caught Janine's hair as she walked past the polar bear exhibit. She was enjoying this beautiful sunny day at the zoo with her two handsome, attentive men. She was finding she really loved Liam's company.

She walked toward the ramp that led to the viewing area that would allow them to see the bears from beneath the surface of the water. She loved watching the polar bears swimming.

The breeze caught the skirt of her floral sundress and blew it upward, flashing a lot of leg. Sloan and Liam grinned as she grasped the fabric and pushed it back down before it revealed everything beneath, which wasn't very much since she'd chosen a skimpy lace thong to wear.

She walked into the cavelike viewpoint and stepped up to the railing in front of the window. A bear swam toward the glass and peered out, then turned and pushed away with his feet.

"He's so cute." She grinned broadly as the bear swam past the window again.

Liam stood beside her and leaned against the railing. "Cute? He's big enough to eat you for lunch."

She hooked her arm around Liam's elbow. "I could say the same about you, but I still think you're cute."

"Ahem." Sloan leaned against the railing on the other side of her.

She laughed and stroked his upper arm. "You, too, Sloan."

Sloan seemed to be handling the situation quite well, but she could sense the seething jealousy just below the surface. On the other hand, she was pretty sure Liam could not. She'd wager Sloan hadn't told Liam about his feelings for her—in case it didn't work out between them, no doubt.

And it probably wouldn't, she thought sadly. She hated the idea of disillusioning Sloan about what might be between them—of dragging him through this emotional roller-coaster ride—but it was the only way to make him see. To convince him to let go of his fantasy about where this relationship might go. She and Sloan were two very different people with very different ideas about dating and sex.

She glanced at his profile as he watched two bears swimming by the glass and her heart ached. A long-term relationship between them simply would not work, and if they fooled themselves into thinking it would, Sloan would get hurt.

And so would she.

On the other hand, Liam seemed like he could handle her lifestyle quite well. And they certainly seemed to be hitting it off. She would definitely have to tread carefully here. Sloan might have introduced Liam into the relationship, probably in an attempt to keep some kind of control over the situation, but when Sloan finally realized that a relationship would not work between them, would he be able to handle her continuing to see his friend?

"You know, speaking of lunch, how about we find somewhere to grab a bite?" Liam suggested.

"Great idea." Sloan gazed at Janine. "What do you think?"

Janine smiled. "Let's go."

As soon as they opened the door of the restaurant, Sloan felt the cool air on his face. A hostess approached them.

"Three?" she asked.

"That's right," Sloan said.

The hostess picked up some menus and led Sloan, Janine, and Liam to a booth.

"Do you think we could have that one?" Janine asked, pointing to a curved booth in the corner.

"Of course." The hostess set the menus on the table and retreated.

"You guys go ahead," Janine said. "I'll be right back."

Liam watched the sweet sway of her hips as she walked toward the ladies' room.

"Janine is sensational." Liam sat on the bench seat. "Thanks for sharing, buddy."

Sloan simply nodded as he sat down, then studied the menu, gritting his teeth.

Janine returned a moment later and grinned. "How about I sit between you?"

Liam stood up and Janine slid onto the bench seat next to Sloan, her soft hip bumping against him, then her warm thigh pressing the length of his. Liam sat on the other side of her.

Janine leaned toward Liam and pulled something out of her purse and showed it to him. Sloan couldn't see what it was.

"I got a surprise for Sloan," she said as she pushed something into Liam's hand. "Do you think he'll like it?"

Liam grinned broadly. "Oh, I'm sure he will."

She turned and grinned at Sloan. "Should have him guess what it is?"

"I think you should give him a hint."

"I think you're right." She grasped Sloan's hand and guided it under the table.

Resting it on her thigh, his fingertips against the fabric of her dress, she drew her skirt upward. Sloan's cock swelled in anticipation as he felt the fabric glide away, then silky skin under his fingertips.

Then she guided his hand to her inner thigh . . . and upward.

When he reached the top . . . Ah, damn, there were no panties. Just silky, moist folds of skin. His finger glided along the soft skin, and he found her slit. Soft. Wet. Hot.

She smiled at him. Damn, she wanted him to do this right here in the restaurant? At the feel of her aroused flesh, he couldn't resist. His finger glided inside her. She drew in a deep breath, then released it slowly. Sloan wanted to capture those full, soft lips of hers.

Janine's hand found the growing bulge in Sloan's pants and stroked. Beside her, Liam settled back and Sloan was pretty sure she was stroking his erection, too.

When he felt her tug on the tag of his zipper, he stilled her hand.

"Maybe we should skip lunch," he murmured.

As soon as Sloan's front door closed behind them, Janine turned to Liam and flung her arms around him. He captured her mouth in a passionate kiss. She drove her tongue between his lips and explored his hot mouth, aware of the warmth of Sloan's body beside her as he watched. Liam's tongue tangled with hers and they undulated together.

Her nipples ached as they jutted against his hard, muscular chest.

"You know, you don't have any panties on," Liam murmured hoarsely once he released her lips.

She tugged open several of his shirt buttons and dragged her fingers over his sculpted chest, then over his abs. God, he was ripped. All solid man.

She felt Sloan's presence behind her, and his hand glided over her ass. As her hand slid lower on Liam, she found Sloan behind her with her other hand, and her fingers found the bulge in the front of Sloan's pants and she stroked it. He drew her flared skirt upward, his hand gliding up her naked thigh, then he palmed her ass. As Sloan stroked around and around, Liam cupped her breast. His thumb stroked over her hard nipple and she sucked in a breath. Sloan's fingers slid under her ass, then between her thighs, and stroked her wet slit.

She leaned forward into Liam's hand, pushing her ass a little higher. Sloan cupped her mound, then nuzzled her neck and stroked between her legs.

"You two are making me so hot." She nuzzled under Liam's chin.

"God, woman, what do you think you're doing to us?" Liam took her hand—which she just realized she'd let pause at his belt—and dragged it over the bulge in his pants.

He unzipped and she pushed her hand into his fly and past his cotton boxers, to wrap her fingers around his straining erection. Such soft skin, stretched taut over solid steel.

Sloan also unzipped and she found his huge member, too. A hard cock in each hand. She squeezed them in delight.

Both of the men dropped their pants to the floor. She turned between them and lowered herself to a crouch, then stared at the two big erections in front of her.

"They're both so big!" She smiled as she stroked them both up and down. "Move closer together."

They moved side to side. She leaned forward and licked Liam's tip, then Sloan's. She wrapped her lips around Sloan and took his cockhead into her mouth. He filled her so full. She squeezed and sucked a little, then released him and moved to Liam's. She took him in her mouth, then slid down his shaft, taking him all the way in. Then she glided off.

"God, it's cold without you, baby," Liam said.

She lifted both cocks upward and licked Sloan from balls to tip, then Liam. Back and forth, like two big lollipop treats. She stroked Sloan's balls while she grasped Liam's cock and licked it all over, then took it in her mouth again and swallowed it whole. She moved up and down on him, squeezing him in her mouth until he moaned in delight. Then she glided away and stroked him with her hand as she grasped Sloan's cock and swallowed his cockhead in her mouth. She swirled her tongue around the tip, then took him deeper and squeezed his shaft inside her mouth.

Finally, she glided away and stroked him, too. Sloan drew her to her feet and captured her mouth, his tongue filling her, then driving in and out. Liam moved behind her and nuzzled the back of her neck. The erotic sensation set her hairs on end and tingles quivered through her. Liam's hands glided around her waist and he drew her tight to his body, the length of his big cock pushing against her behind. Sloan stroked her breasts, leaned down and captured a nipple in his mouth, then sucked. She moaned at the intense sensations spiraling through her.

She grabbed Sloan's huge cock and stroked as he licked and teased her sensitive nipples.

He buried his face between her breasts and moaned as she squeezed his cock.

"Oh, God, sweetheart, I want to be inside you," Sloan said.

She took his hand and guided it downward until he stroked his fingers over her very wet slit.

"I feel the same way," she murmured huskily.

"The ottoman." Liam stepped back and took her hand, then led her into the living room.

She sat down on the burgundy leather ottoman and cupped her breasts, then stroked them. Both men watched, their eyes darkening. She stroked down her stomach, then glided her fingers over her slit.

"You two have made me so wet." She stroked over her slick flesh, watching their twitching cocks. She slid a finger inside herself and Liam groaned, his hand gliding along his cock.

Sloan dropped to his knees in front of her and clamped his mouth over her nipple and sucked deeply. She moaned at the exquisite pleasure. His hand covered hers and he stroked her slick flesh. Then his finger joined hers inside.

"I need to fuck you right now," Sloan said.

She widened her legs in clear invitation. Sloan pressed his cockhead to her opening and drove inside her. She gasped at the intense invasion of his massive cock.

Liam stood beside them and she grasped his cock and drew it to her mouth. She swallowed his cock and squeezed it with her mouth. Sloan cupped her breasts and drew back, then thrust into her again. She moaned around Liam's cock, then gripped his shaft tightly in her hand as she continued to suck.

Sloan drew back again, the dragging of his wide cockhead against her inner passage sending pleasure thrumming through her.

"God, I'm going to come." Sloan drove into her again, then began thrusting in earnest.

In and out, filling her again and again. She sucked on

Liam until the pleasure exploded inside her and she squeezed Sloan's huge cock and moaned. He kept on thrusting. Deep. Hard. She wailed as the orgasm ricocheted through her. Sloan thrust hard again, then rocked against her. She felt his liquid heat fill her as she clung to his shoulders, still riding the wave of ecstasy.

Finally, Sloan collapsed on top of her, sucking in air. She loved the feel of his big, solid body on her, but she knew he held off much of his weight with his arms, his hands pressed on the top of the ottoman on both sides of her. She opened her eyes and saw Liam standing there, his cock still rock hard above her face.

She kissed Sloan's cheek and he turned his face to capture her mouth in a kiss. Tender and sweet. He released her lips and his loving gaze washed over her. Warming her. Sending butterflies through her stomach.

He pushed himself to his feet and she smiled up at Liam as he moved into place and knelt before her. He pressed his cock to her opening and slid inside. She wrapped her legs around his hips and drew him tight to her.

She raised her lips and he kissed her. There was a sweetness to the gentle brush of his lips, too, which surprised her.

"Make me come again, Liam."

He smiled. "I'll do my best."

He thrust deep and she knew his best would be pretty damned good. She arched against him, and he drew back and thrust again. She moaned as another orgasm swelled inside her. He thrust into her like a piston, filling her again and again. She squeezed him inside as his hand slipped between them and found her clit. He stroked it and her insides fluttered wildly.

He slammed into her again and again, stroking her clit at the same time. She clung to him, then wailed as she flew off into ecstasy.

Sloan held Janine close to him, his arms wrapped around her possessively. Their naked bodies were pressed tightly together, her soft round behind tucked against his groin as they spooned. He was intensely aware of Liam lying on the other side of Janine, his face only inches from hers.

Damn it. He'd thought that he could bring Liam along for Janine's fantasy, enabling himself to score points with her for stepping it up a notch and embracing her adventurous lifestyle, while gaining some level of control of the situation. But he hadn't thought through the repercussions. He'd figured Liam was a good choice for a sexy stranger, but it wasn't supposed to go beyond that.

Sloan nuzzled his face in Janine's soft hair, breathing in her herbal scent. Leave it to Janine to throw him off balance by inviting Liam to join them for the day. If he'd thought about it, he could have predicted she'd do something like that. Now the problem was, she seemed to have taken a liking to Liam. And that meant that Liam was continuing to be a part of their sexual adventures.

He gazed at his friend's face in the moonlight. If Sloan asked Liam to back off, he would. Sloan knew that. But that could get Sloan into more trouble in the long run. Janine would be majorly ticked off if she thought Sloan was trying to control whom she was involved with.

Either way, he didn't want to admit to Liam that he had

feelings for Janine. He didn't like sharing his feelings with others. It was hard enough sharing them with Janine. He hated showing that kind of vulnerability to anyone.

Bottom line was, bringing Liam into the situation had scored him points with Janine. It had also helped distract her from the other men she was seeing. Anything he could do to weaken those ties helped put him in a better position.

So keeping Liam involved was probably the best thing for Sloan.

He snuggled closer to Janine. If it came down to it, Sloan should be able to win in a competition with Liam, because he had love on his side. That was his secret weapon. Not that Liam would really compete with him if Sloan broke down and admitted his feelings for her. But he wouldn't do that unless he really had to.

If he could just find a way to spend some one-on-one time with her, to show how right he was for her, then he was sure he could win her over.

Twelve

Janine glanced up from the computer screen when Rebecca, her secretary, stepped into her office and closed the door behind her.

"Janine. There's someone here to see you. He's absolutely gorgeous and I'm so jealous! Do you want me to send him in?"

Janine's lips quirked. "Well, I'm not going to refuse after that description, am I?"

"Good choice." Rebecca opened the door and smiled at someone. "Ms. Reid will see you now." Rebecca smiled.

Sloan stepped into the doorway and leaned against the doorjamb. "Hi."

"Hi. This is a surprise."

He grinned. "A pleasant one, I hope."

Rebecca just stood gazing at him, a half smile on her lips.

"Rebecca, why don't you go for lunch?"

Rebecca glanced at her, then back to Sloan. "Okay, boss. I'll see you around one." She slipped past Sloan, a wistful look in her eyes. Clearly, she would love to be the one dating Sloan, and for some reason, a pang of jealousy surged through Janine.

Sloan stepped farther into the office. "Actually, it's such a beautiful day, I came to invite you out for lunch. I was hoping you could steal a couple of hours from work."

"Your schedule's clear, boss," Rebecca called from the outer office. "That should be no problem."

"Thanks, Rebecca. Now go to lunch."

"Okay, I'm gone," she called back.

Janine waited until she heard Rebecca's desk drawer open and close as she retrieved her purse, and then Janine watched as Rebecca walked down the hall.

"She's cute," Sloan said.

"You think so? Want me to invite her on our next date?"

Sloan glanced her way in surprise. "Really?"

"No, not really. She's my secretary. I'm sure there's some sort of sexual harassment problem if I even suggest it."

"Oh."

She smiled. "Don't look so crestfallen. If you'd like me to invite another woman along, I know someone you would probably find attractive who would enjoy joining in."

He stared at her, and his vivid blue eyes darkened. He pushed the door closed and walked around her desk, then turned her chair to face him. Janine gazed up at him as he towered over her.

Sloan took her hand and pulled her to her feet and into his arms. "As tempting as that sounds—and believe me, the thought of being with two sexy women at the same time is a definite fantasy of mine—I only want to be with you."

Janine choked back a lump in her throat. She'd really thought Sloan would jump at a chance like that—to be with two women. But the intensity of his piercing blue gaze as it held hers, the confident, absolute certainty of his conviction that he wanted her, and her alone, melted her heart. Right at this moment, if she let them, tears would spring from her eyes at the sincerity of his love for her.

Oh, God, no. Not love. Some misguided attraction or desire to recapture what they might have had when they were younger. But he was not in love with her. She didn't believe that.

She couldn't believe that.

He captured her lips in a compelling combination of tenderness and authority. His tongue swept into her mouth, engaging hers in a tumultuous dance. When he finally released her, she simply gazed at him, catching her breath.

"So? Lunch?"

"Um . . . sure." She grabbed her purse and pulled it from her drawer. "What do you have in mind? One of the outdoor patios on the river?"

"No. Something more interesting than that." He crossed her office and opened the door.

"More interesting? Like what?"

"Follow me and you'll find out."

"Oh, a surprise?" She wasn't sure if she wanted a surprise, especially from Sloan. But she was committed now as she followed him to the elevator.

She stepped off at the lobby and she followed him out the front door, then down the street. He stopped in front of a big black motorcycle.

"I didn't know you rode a motorcycle."

"There's a lot about me you don't know." He unlocked the case at the back and pulled out a helmet, which he handed to her.

She pulled on the helmet, then glanced down at her straight black skirt. "Hmm."

He chuckled as he pulled on a black leather jacket he'd stowed in the storage compartment. "What? My wild and passionate Janine is going to let a little thing like a skirt stop her from enjoying an adventure with a man?"

She compressed her lips and grabbed the sides of her skirt, wriggling it up a little, then climbed onto the backseat of the big machine. A couple of young guys passing by whistled at her show of leg.

Sloan glanced at her black-stocking-clad thighs in appreciation, then climbed onto the bike in front of her.

"Hang on." He thrust his leg down and the machine rumbled to life.

She wrapped her arms around his waist, her fingers gliding over the supple leather of his jacket. Sloan pulled into the noontime traffic and zoomed down the road. About ten minutes later, the bike zipped along the highway. Janine rested her head against Sloan's back, protecting her face from the wind.

After about a twenty-minute ride, he pulled off on a small side road, which got smaller as they followed it through trees, until finally it petered off into a dirt road. Still he drove until finally he took another side road. Janine could see the glitter of water ahead.

He pulled off the road to a clearing in the trees with the banks of the lake only yards away, then turned off the engine.

"It's pretty isolated, so I thought it would be the perfect place for a picnic."

The clear blue sky above and the sunlight glittering on the calm water made a beautiful view.

"It's lovely."

He got off the bike, and she took the hand he offered to help her climb down.

"I packed some sandwiches and juice," he said.

As he stepped forward to retrieve the lunch, she stepped in his path. "You know, why don't we forget about eating right now?" She stroked her hand over his shoulder, then down the front of his leather jacket. Her fingers caught the zipper tab and she dragged it down. Slowly.

"I can think of something else I'd much rather do right now than have lunch."

She flattened her other hand on his solid chest and caressed. The feel of hard muscle under her palm sent thrills through her. The zipper tag hit the end and his jacket fell open. He shrugged it off, then tugged off his black T-shirt.

"Well, there's an offer I can't refuse," he said.

Her gaze fell to the tanned flesh of his bulging arms and broad chest, and traveled down to his ridged abs. She smiled and pressed him back against the bike, then ran her hand over his bulging crotch. She glanced around. No one was anywhere in sight, and they were so far off the beaten path she was sure no one would happen upon them.

She unfastened his black leather belt and unzipped his jeans. His erection had pushed past the waistband of his boxers, and several inches of cock peeked over the edge. She tucked her fingers under the waistband and drew it down, exposing the top half of his shaft.

He kicked off his shoes, then pushed his jeans and boxers down in one motion and stepped out of them. Now he stood before her naked except for his socks. And she was fully clothed. It was an incredibly sexy situation.

Her fingertips brushed against the satin skin of his shaft, and she wrapped her fingers around it. Of course, he was so thick she couldn't close her fingers around him. She stroked up and down, loving the feel of his big, marble-hard member in her hand.

"How sturdy is that bike?" she asked. "On the stand, I mean."

He grinned. "It'll hold both our weights without falling down, if that's what you're asking."

"That's exactly what I'm asking."

He wrapped his hands around her hips, pulled her to him, and kissed her, his mouth caressing hers with passion. She felt his fingers at her back, then he glided her skirt down, revealing her black pantyhose.

"You seemed to be having some difficulty with your skirt on the way here, so I wanted you to be comfortable."

She grinned. "I see." She stepped out of her shoes and tugged off her pantyhose, then unfastened her blouse buttons, one by one.

He watched as her blouse parted bit by bit, slowly revealing her black lace bra beneath. She dropped her blouse to the ground, leaving her standing there in only her bra and matching panties.

He kicked his leg over the bike and sat on the passenger seat, which rose above the driver's seat, then lifted her onto the bike facing him. She leaned back and ran her hands over her breasts, then squeezed them together. Sloan's gaze locked on them as they swelled forward, and he watched her hands as they stroked over her shoulders and then down her arms, as she caressed herself seductively. She hooked her thumbs under her bra straps, then glided up and down. She dropped one strap off her shoulder, then the other. He watched as she stroked down her stomach, her other hand cupping her breast and squeezing. When her hand reached her panties, she tucked a finger under the waistband, then lifted. Sloan's cock twitched and he wrapped his hand around it. Gazing at his gigantic member, she tucked her hand inside the crotch of her panties and stroked.

Sloan could just imagine what Janine felt inside the tiny little panties of hers. If her pussy was half as wet as his cock was hard, she must be ready to come right now. Her hand glided out of her panties and back up to her breasts, her fingers glistening in the sunlight.

She stroked over her breasts again and squeezed them together. They swelled forward enticingly. She toyed with her loose bra straps, then tugged downward, pulling the cups a little. She tugged the lace lower and his breath caught as her nipple appeared above the black fabric. She pulled the other cup down and her other nipple peeked out. He tightened his hold on his cock.

She reached around behind her and unfastened her bra, then held it against her breasts. She stroked her hands over the cups, then lowered the garment slowly, revealing more and more of her perfect breasts. Finally, she tossed it aside.

She wrapped her hands around her waist, her arms pushing her breasts upward, then stroked their undersides.

She leaned back against the instrument panel, caressing her breasts, then her shoulders, back to her breasts . . . her hands constantly moving, touching, squeezing.

"God, Janine, I'm so hard."

She smiled. "I can see that. Do you like watching me touch myself?"

"Absolutely."

"Then why aren't you stroking your cock? I'd like to watch you stroke it."

Of course she would. He had assumed otherwise, but he should have figured Janine out by now. He glided his hand up and down his cock, enjoying the hungry look in her topaz blue eyes. She stroked over her breasts, her hands moving in circles. Then she licked her finger and toyed with one nipple. The tight dusky bud glistened with moisture and he longed to suck it into his mouth.

"I want to see you touch your pussy again."

She smiled and slid one hand down her flat stomach while the other hand continued to stroke her hard nipple. He watched her fingers glide under her panties, the lacy fabric moving. She drew her hand out again, then tucked her fingers under the waistband of her panties and drew them down the sides of her hips, lower and lower, but keeping her pussy covered. She coiled around and knelt on the bike, her back to him, and lowered the back of her panties, baring her luscious ass. She dragged the small lacy item down her thighs, wiggled them over her knees, and then along her calves and off. She crumpled the lacy fabric in her hand and stroked it over the curve of her behind, then around her hip. When she seductively turned back to face him, she held the scrap of lace over her pussy as her legs parted until she sat astride the seat again. She stroked the panties in circles between her legs, then glided upward. His gaze locked on her sweet little pussy, the furry star above, as she caressed her breasts with the black lace. Round and round. She dragged the fabric down her stomach again and over her intimate folds. Finally, she tossed the lace toward him. The panties hooked on his throbbing cock. He grabbed them and stroked them over his hard flesh.

"Mmm. Very nice." She watched as he caressed his shaft up and down with her tiny panties. "You know, it's so sunny out and I have so much flesh exposed. Do you have any suntan lotion?"

He reached into the black bag affixed to the bike, tugged out a spray bottle of sunscreen, and handed it to her.

"A pump. Nice." She sprayed the lotion across her breasts and down her stomach. More and more until a thick white coat covered her. She stroked her hands over her breasts, around and around, spreading the lotion until her breasts shone in the sunlight like polished marble, then down her stomach, leaving a sheen. Finally, her fingers glided over her pussy and dipped inside.

Sloan's cock ached with the need to drive inside her.

"Sweetheart, you're driving me insane."

She smiled. "Really?" Her hips shifted from side to side as she shimmied toward him on the leather seat.

She dragged her finger over the tip of his cock. The intense sensations rocketed through him. He wanted to grab her by the waist and lift her onto his raging cock right now.

She leaned forward and licked his cockhead and he groaned.

"You have such a big cock, Sloan. I really had no idea."

"So if you'd known, would you have agreed to go out with me sooner?"

She grinned. "Well, you never know."

She pressed her lips against him, then surrounded his cockhead with her hot, wet mouth.

"Oh, yeah." His hand cupped her head.

He drew her hair back from her face, coiling the long strands around his hand. She glided forward, taking his shaft deeper into her warmth. Then her head bobbed back and forth, his hand gliding with her. She tucked her hands under his balls and caressed. He moaned at the delightful sensation. He drew her head forward and she opened wide, taking him deeper. Amazingly deep.

She squeezed him in her mouth and he groaned.

"Oh, damn. I'm so fucking close."

Her hand tightened on his balls, gently, and she glided off his cock.

"Then come. Right now." She covered his cockhead and wrapped her hot mouth tight around it. She sucked as her fingers stroked behind his testicles.

He burst in her mouth, groaning out loud at the exquisite release. She stroked his exposed shaft as she continued to suck him.

Finally, he collapsed back on the bike, his cock still protruding from her mouth. She glided off his tip and smiled.

Janine gazed at Sloan's slumped form. God, it was hot watching him come. Feeling him erupt in her mouth.

He drew in a deep breath, then smiled broadly. "Now it's your turn."

She gazed at his wilted cock. "It doesn't look like you're quite ready." She dragged her fingers over her slick folds, longing for his hard erection inside her.

He leaned forward and stroked his hands over her breasts, still slick from the sunscreen. He cupped them with his big hands and caressed, sending tingles through her, then dragged his fingertips over her nipples. Her insides melted with intense desire. He leaned closer and captured one hard nipple in his mouth. His tongue teased over the tip, then he sucked. She moaned at the sharp sensation. She wrapped her hands around his head, her fingers forking through his hair, and she pulled him tight to her breast. He teased and cajoled her hard bud with his tongue. Then he sucked again and she cried out.

He chuckled, then continued to lick her nipple as he dragged one hand down her stomach, then over her folds. He glided over her clit and electric bursts pulsed across her nerve endings. His fingers stroked her slit then slid inside. Her pelvis arched upward and she squeezed him, longing for something longer and thicker than his fingers.

She gazed at his semierect cock with longing. She swung her leg over the bike and leaned over it, her breasts tucked over the side of the driver's seat. She opened her legs and stroked her round behind.

Sloan took her hint and climbed off the bike, then stood behind her.

"Wow. What a beautiful view."

His hands joined hers, caressing her behind. He glided between her cheeks and down, stroking her slit. She sucked in a deep breath and cupped her breasts, then stroked them, tweaking the nipples as he found her clit and teased it.

"Oh, God, Sloan. I want you inside me."

He chuckled. "Sweetheart, I love hearing you say that."

His fingers glided into her, then she felt hard flesh nudge against her.

"God, Sloan, if that's your cock, drive it into me. Right now."

An agony of pleasure ripped through her as he drove deep into her in one sudden thrust, his broad cock stretching her wide. She wailed at the intensity of his sublime invasion.

"Ohhh . . . yes. Fuck me now. Deep and hard."

He drew back, the ridge of his cockhead stroking her insides. She quivered. He drove forward again and she moaned. He drew back.

"Sloan . . . yes . . . Please fuck me faster."

He thrust deep, then kept on thrusting. Faster and faster. She sucked in air, then wailed as pleasure burst through her in an intense wave. His cock plunged into her over and over. She gasped, then cried out again. And again. He exploded inside her, catapulting her into ecstasy.

Finally, she collapsed on the bike, Sloan's body pressed tight to hers, both of them gasping for air.

She pushed away loose strands of hair from her face. "That was incredibly hot," she panted.

"You're not kidding." He nuzzled her neck, then kissed her temple.

Her heart melted at the incredibly tender gesture. He was so sweet. So . . . loving.

It almost scared her.

He cupped her shoulders and stood up, drawing her with him. He turned her around and kissed her, his lips moving on hers in a persuasive, tender manner. She melted against him, totally aware of their naked bodies touching so intimately. Not in a sexual sense, but like a man and woman. In a real relationship.

Like two people in love.

Oh, God, she couldn't fall in love with Sloan. And she certainly didn't want him falling in love with her. They were all wrong for each other.

At least, he was wrong for her. He was having fun playing the part, but she knew he'd never fully accept the way she was, allowing her the total freedom she needed.

Damn, she had made a big mistake agreeing to date him. Now that she'd tasted what it was like to make love with him . . . God, he was addictive. Could she really be as selfish as she felt like being right now? Wanting to continue this relationship with him because of the sensational sex?

On the other hand, he was a big boy. *Oh, God, really big!*

She sucked in a breath. The point was, Sloan would never give up on the idea of having a romantic relationship with her until he came face-to-face with the fact that she would never settle for a traditional relationship—one woman, one man. It felt too much like a domination scenario. Not that she minded domination, as long as she could walk away from it at any time.

No, she would not regret agreeing to date Sloan. It was the only way for him to understand what she required in a relationship and to come to terms with it. He would eventually realize he would never convince her to settle for anything less than total freedom.

Sloan sensed a change in her. After their incredible lovemaking, all alone out here in the wilderness, he had felt closer to her than ever before. There had been an intimacy between them. Just the two of them, exulting in pleasuring each other. Then their tender kiss.

Then suddenly she'd withdrawn, even though she hadn't moved a muscle.

He lingered over the kiss a little longer before finally releasing her lips.

Something flickered in her topaz eyes, then she smiled. "How about those sandwiches? I'm incredibly hungry after that great workout."

"Sure." He released her and fetched the bagged lunch from the storage compartment on the bike, feeling a deep sense of loss as she pulled on her clothes.

A knock sounded, and Sloan crossed to his front door and opened it.

Derek stood on the other side. "Hi."

"Hey. Come on in." Sloan stepped back to let him in.

Derek stepped into Sloan's house and Sloan gestured toward the couch. Derek crossed the room and sat down.

"So, where's our girl?" Derek asked.

"The other room. I'll let her know you're here."

He walked down the hall and opened the bedroom door. At the sight of Janine standing in front of the mirror, brushing her long blond hair, wearing only a sexy red lace thong and matching bra, he smiled. His gaze glided over her delightfully round behind to the black stockings with sexy lace edges on the top—which somehow stayed up on their own without a garter belt—then lingered on her bare white thighs above. His cock stirred.

"You look sensational."

She smiled at him in the mirror. "Thank you." She put down the brush and turned around. Her breasts spilled over the top of the lace cups in a most enticing way. "Is Derek here?"

"Yes, he just arrived."

She picked up her black coat from the bed and pulled it on. His eyebrows arched. "Are you leaving?"

She laughed. "No way. I just thought I'd give you both a little show."

"I thought I was in charge tonight."

Janine's penchant for handcuffs and her teasing about him dominating her had given him the idea for tonight's scenario. Since she insisted on interacting with other men in addition to him, at least if he was the one calling the shots, he could maintain a level of control. That actually made the situation not only tolerable but exhilarating. Plus, it gave him the opportunity to use a trait she sometimes viewed as a flaw in him to shining advantage.

Her gaze shot to his. "Oh, of course." She walked toward him until she stood facing him, then lowered her gaze. "Whatever you wish . . . Master."

Thirteen

Sloan grinned. "That's more like it. Now let's go entertain our guest."

Janine started to slip the coat off.

"No. Leave it on."

She raised an eyebrow.

"What? A good idea's a good idea," he said.

She laughed, then followed him from the room.

As they walked into the living room, Derek turned his gaze to Janine.

"Janine, this is my friend Derek. You'll be entertaining both of us this evening."

"Yes, Master," she said.

Derek grinned.

Janine crossed to the dance pole Sloan had set up in the corner for this evening. She grabbed it with one hand and twirled around it, sending her coat flaring. Standing behind the pole, she flicked open the single button she'd fastened, then teasingly revealed a long, luscious leg. She twirled around the pole to put her back toward them, then eased the coat down, revealing her lovely shoulders. She peered over one shoulder and smiled at them, then turned to face them again. She held the coat closed over her breasts, then swayed her shoulders and hips from side to side as she eased the coat down slowly, revealing more and more skin. Finally, she let it slip from her shoulders and fall to the floor, leaving her standing in her red lace bra, thong, and black stockings.

She kicked the coat away as she walked around the pole, then faced them again, leaning back against the metal and hugging her body, pushing her breasts together tightly. Sloan's cock twitched—as he was sure Derek's did, too—at the sight of her breasts threatening to pop out of the bra. She swayed back and forth, then turned around and, gazing over her shoulder again, unfastened the bra. The straps fell from her shoulders, and she slipped her arms free. She faced them, holding the bra against herself, then squeezed her breasts together. She glided the bra down, allowing one nipple to peek over the top of the fabric, then the other. Finally, she tossed the bra aside.

"Very nice, Janine. Now go get us some water."

"Water?"

He stifled a grin. Of course she'd be surprised he wanted her to bring water instead of beer or wine.

He raised an eyebrow. "Are you questioning an order?"

"No, Master."

"Good. There's a pitcher of ice water on the counter."

She turned around and headed into the kitchen, then returned carrying a tray with three ice-filled glasses and the full pitcher he'd set out a few minutes earlier. As she leaned over to place it on the table, her breasts swayed enticingly in front of them. Sloan longed to reach out and cup one. To feel the soft mound in his hand.

The ice cubes tinkled against the pitcher as she filled each glass.

"Fine. Now come over here," Sloan said.

She stood in front of him and he stroked along the top of her thong, then dipped his finger under the elastic. He tugged the fabric downward, slowly revealing first the little star shape of her golden pubic hair, then her delightfully shaved pussy. He slipped the thong the rest of the way down and she stepped out of it. He dragged his finger over the little fuzzy star.

"Lovely. Now take your glass and sit in the chair over there."

He'd set an armchair across the room where it was easy to view from the couch and chairs. She picked up her glass and walked to the chair. Sloan's gaze locked on her swaying ass. She sat down, took a sip from her glass, then set it on the small table he'd placed next to the chair.

"Now hook your legs over the armrests."

"Yes, Master."

Both he and Derek watched her as she opened her stocking-clad legs and hooked her knees over the armrests. Sloan couldn't pry his gaze from her naked pussy.

"Lovely. Now I want you to take a cube of ice from your glass and stroke it over your breasts."

She smiled, then dipped her fingers into the icy water and drew out an ice cube. She brought it to her face, water dripping from her fingers and down her chest, and licked the cube. As her tongue lapped out and stroked the hard, slippery cube, Sloan's cock hardened.

Slowly, she drew the cube down her chest, then over her

breast. When she dragged it over the aureola, her nipple hardened immediately. Then she glided it to her other nipple and stroked it with the ice. That one also thrust forward at the cold. Water dribbled down her flesh, dripping over her breast.

The doorbell rang.

Janine hesitated as she glanced at the door, then her gaze shot to Sloan.

"I'll get it." Derek got up and headed for the door.

Janine dropped the ice cube back into the glass, then drew her legs from the armrest and stood up. Derek now stood at the door.

"I didn't say to move," Sloan said as she grabbed her coat. "Now sit back down."

She dropped her coat and sat down again.

"Legs back on the armrests."

She did as she was told, her gaze nervously shooting to the door.

Derek opened the door a little, then turned back to them. "It's the pizza guy."

"Let him in." Sloan smiled as Janine's eyes grew wide.

Derek swung open the door and stepped back.

Janine had to stop herself from racing for the coat and covering herself, or at the very least closing her thighs and covering her breasts. What had gotten into Sloan?

Her cheeks turned crimson as a man carrying a pizza box stepped through the doorway, then closed the door behind him. Then her gaze slid to his face, expecting to see a googly-eyed stranger, but instead she saw a familiar face. Liam.

"I thought you couldn't make it tonight," she said.

When she'd asked Sloan if he would invite Liam tonight, he'd told her Liam wasn't available. She'd wondered if Sloan just didn't want Liam around her. She knew she'd pushed his buttons by inviting Liam to join them for the day after their incredible stranger fantasy, and Sloan had definitely been a bit jealous of the other man, but it seemed Sloan was handling it better than she thought.

Liam's gaze fell on her breasts, then glided down her torso, to her exposed folds.

He grinned. "The pizza man is always available for delivery, ma'am."

Sloan stood up and pulled out his wallet and peered inside. "Hmm. I was sure I had enough money for the pizza. What about you, Derek?"

Derek shook his head. "I didn't bring any cash with me."

Liam glanced from Derek to Sloan, his eyebrows raised.

"We don't have any money, but"—Sloan glanced toward Janine—"I'm sure Janine would be willing to pay you."

Liam gazed at Janine again. "The young lady doesn't seem to have any money on her."

"I wasn't thinking of money," Sloan said.

"Really?" Liam thrust the pizza box into Derek's hands.

He walked toward her, his gaze on her thrusting nipples. He stood in front of her and stroked her shoulder, then down her chest to her breasts.

He cupped it and squeezed. "Gorgeous."

He stroked both her breasts, then teased her nipples, sending tingles dancing through her straight from the tips of her breasts to her vagina.

"This certainly is my lucky day," Liam said.

Crouching in front of her, he gazed at her exposed pussy. Then he glided his fingers downward and stroked her slit.

"I don't know what you guys were doing before I got here, but she's wet and ready."

He stood up and unzipped his jeans, then brought out his big, erect cock. He stepped close to her and held it in his hand, the tip only inches from her face.

She leaned forward and licked his big cockhead. Then she stroked it with her fingertips. He released it and she wrapped her fingers around it, then stroked forward and back a couple of times.

"Your cock is so big and hard."

He chuckled.

She wrapped her lips around it and drew it into her mouth. Her other hand scooped his balls and fondled them while she glided down on his big cock, taking it deep into her mouth. She stroked and sucked and squeezed his balls. He groaned in appreciation. A quick glance to the other men and she saw they'd taken out their own cocks and were stroking them. She glided one hand around behind him and cupped his hard, firm butt. The feel of his erection in her mouth, and knowing Derek and Sloan were turned-on by watching her, aroused her immensely.

She drew back, her mouth squeezing Liam as she moved, her hand firmly around his shaft at the base. She swirled her tongue around his cockhead, then dove down on him again, taking him all the way. He groaned and his fingers raked through her long hair. She bobbed up and down, sucking and squeezing, cradling his balls in her hand. They grew firm and he stiffened, then groaned his release as he erupted into her mouth. She stroked his muscular butt as he twitched to completion, then drew back. He grinned down at her and winked.

"That was great. I'll deliver pizza here anytime." Liam caressed her breast, then tucked his spent cock into his pants and zipped up.

Sloan walked toward her and handed her a piece of pizza on a paper plate. She took it and began to eat, her legs still resting on the armrests, leaving her totally exposed. Liam grabbed a piece of pizza and sat on the couch with the other two men, all gazing at her open legs as they ate. Derek put down his empty plate and walked toward the kitchen.

Sloan's hot gaze on her melting slit sent her hormones spiraling through her.

The doorbell rang again.

Janine sent Sloan a questioning glance.

"Janine, rest your hands on your knees . . . and widen your legs a little." Sloan walked toward the door.

Okay, he expected her to stay put. Could it be that it was Jonas this time? But she was certain Derek had said Jonas wouldn't be in town this weekend.

Would Sloan really open the door to a stranger with her sitting here naked and fully exposed like this?

He opened the door and peered out. "Ah, the beer man." He swung the door wide and Derek stood on the doorstep, holding a case of beer.

Derek must have slipped out the back door from the kitchen.

Sloan let him in and closed the door. Derek set the case of beer on the floor.

"Sorry, I have no money to pay, but"—Sloan glanced toward Janine—"you might be interested in an alternate form of payment."

Derek's eyes twinkled as he glanced at Janine and feigned surprise at seeing a naked woman blatantly exposing herself across the room.

"I'm in." Derek tore open the top of the beer case and pulled one out, then strode toward her.

He opened the brown bottle and took a swig as his hot gaze raked over her. He placed the bottle on the side table, then crouched in front of her and cupped her breasts. His right hand was cold, and her nipple peaked against his palm. He picked up the bottle again and touched it to the tip of her nipple. The nipple nearly exploded with sensation as the stinging cold sent hot tingles through her. He dragged the bottle across her chest to her other breast and then over the nipple. Need quivered through her.

He leaned forward and took one cold nipple into his hot mouth. She nearly cried out at the intense sensation. He sucked and she dropped her head back and moaned. The cold bottle touched her skin again as he dragged it down her stomach, then pressed it against her hot, moist flesh. She moaned again. He stroked it up and down her slit. Cold, moist glass against her hot, soft opening.

His finger found her clit and he gave it a featherlight stroke. The bottom edge of the beer bottle pushed against her opening as he continued to stroke her tiny button. She gazed across the room at Sloan with hunger in her eyes. Derek crouched down and licked the condensation, which had dripped onto her stomach from the bottle, then glided lower, the bottle still pressed against her slit. His tongue found her clit and she moaned and arched forward. He drew the bottle from her flesh and grinned. Heat suffused her once again as she watched him lick her juices from the glass. He put it down on the table again, then rested his hands on her knees and held her legs wide. He leaned forward and licked her slit, and she moaned at the incredible sensation.

He drew back and reached for the beer bottle again, then took a sip. Then he leaned forward and wrapped his lips around her clit. She gasped as cold liquid washed against her sensitive nub as he took it into his beer-filled mouth. Then he sucked and licked her. He dragged his cold lips down her slit, then covered her with his mouth and pressed his cold tongue inside her. She grabbed his head and clung to his thick black hair as he pulsed inside her. He drew back and grinned at her, then stroked her slit with two fingers and slid them inside her wet passage. She squeezed his fingers as she arched forward. He clamped his mouth over her clit and began to lick and suck as his fingers glided in and out of her. Pleasure washed through her, then sputtered out of control as an orgasm swept over her. She dropped her head back and moaned. Long and loud as he kept stroking her insides and sucking on her clit.

Finally, she slumped back, spent. He drew back and smiled, then stroked lightly over her breasts before he stood up.

"That was definitely the best payment I've ever had." He crossed to the couch and sat down again.

Sloan couldn't drag his gaze from Janine, her legs wide, her pussy glistening from the slickness of her arousal. Her face, as Derek had sent her to orgasm, had blossomed into a blissful expression that lit his heart. He loved seeing her in pleasure . . . even when it was another man giving it to her. There was an easy intimacy between Janine and Derek.

Sloan knew they weren't in love—that was clear—but

they liked each other a lot and respected each other. From what Derek had told him, the two of them were close friends. When Janine had a problem she had to talk through, she'd go to Derek. If Derek needed another viewpoint, he'd go to Janine. They helped each other and cared about each other. Sloan thought he'd be jealous, wanting Janine to do those things with him and him alone, but that was unrealistic. Everyone needed friends. Another perspective. Another person to depend on. The fact that Derek was a man rather than a girlfriend shouldn't matter.

Except for the sex part. But he didn't really think Derek was competition in the romance department.

And, when it came right down to it, it was fucking exciting to watch Derek make her come.

"Hey, Sloan, keep staring like that and you're going to burn a hole through the woman," Liam said.

Fourteen

Sloan jerked his gaze from Janine, realizing he'd been staring hard at her dripping pussy the whole time.

"Maybe you want to instruct your sub to entertain us," Derek suggested.

"Great idea." Sloan took a sip of his beer. "Janine, stroke those beautiful breasts of yours."

She sat up a little, her legs still draped over the armrests, and cupped her breasts, then lifted them. Her thumbs swirled over her hardening nipples. She reached toward the table at her side and drew an ice cube from the water, then dragged the dripping cube over her right nipple. Sloan watched the nub protrude forward and water dribbled down her breast, then over her stomach.

She glided the ice cube over her other nipple, which also swelled. The water dribbling down her stomach trickled through the fuzzy star, then down to her already wet slit.

Sloan's cock rose. "Now tease that pretty little pussy."

One of her hands stroked down her flat stomach and over

the star. She petted it with her fingertips for a few seconds, then stroked lower. Sloan's cock throbbed as she glided her fingertips over her slit, back and forth, her fingers glazing with moisture. When she slid her finger inside her opening, he grasped his cock and stroked, longing to be inside her.

"Come over here." Sloan's words sounded coarse and needy.

She stood up and walked toward him, a gentle sway to her hips. When she stood in front of him, he reached for her lovely breasts and cupped them, loving the feel of her hard nipples driving into his palms. He stroked, then glided his hands downward. He ran his fingers over her delightfully wet slit, then pulled the folds apart with his thumbs and leaned close to her, her musky scent like an aphrodisiac, filling him with compelling need.

He licked her slit, loving her sweet womanly taste, then drove his tongue into her. She sucked in a breath. He leaned back and simply stared at her lovely pussy, then glided his thumbs over the folds at the front, drawing them apart until he could see her little clit. He dabbed his tongue against it, then flicked from side to side. Her breathing accelerated and she grasped his head, her fingers raking through his hair.

He licked her clit, then drew back. He didn't want her to come yet.

He glanced along the couch. Both Liam and Derek had huge erections towering from their jeans.

"I think we should all get naked." Derek stood up and dropped his jeans to the floor. He kicked them aside, then started unfastening his shirt buttons.

Liam stood up and shed his clothes, too. Janine watched

the naked male chests with hunger. Sloan stood up and undressed, then sat down again.

"Janine, I want you to tease each of our cocks with your wet little pussy, but don't make any of us come."

Janine smiled and walked toward Liam on the other end of the couch. She undulated her body toward him in a seductive rhythm, then wrapped her hand around his erection as she pressed her breasts close to his face. He licked a nipple and she moaned in appreciation. She rested her knees on the couch, on either side of his thighs, and pressed his cockhead to her slick opening. Slowly, she lowered herself onto him, his shaft disappearing inside her. Her gaze locked on Liam's and she smiled as she glided up and down on him for a few strokes. She stood up, then moved to Derek. She undulated in front of him, too, then offered him a breast. A moment later, she pressed his cockhead to her slit and lowered onto it, just as she had with Liam.

Sloan couldn't stop watching that tower of flesh impale her. Then she stepped away from Derek and stood in front of Sloan. Her hips swayed toward him then away several times. She offered him a breast and he covered her nipple, then sucked lightly. She stifled a gasp, then her warm hand wrapped around his aching cock. When her hot wet slit pressed against his tip, he almost moaned aloud. She lowered herself onto him, her tight sheath squeezing him.

He groaned as she took him completely inside her. She captured his gaze and he stared into her topaz eyes as she raised her body, abandoning his hard shaft to the cold air, then lowered herself again. After three strokes, he was afraid he'd explode inside her, but steely determination held him back.

Knowing she would pull away any second, he grasped her

hips and held her tight against him, his raging cock twitching inside her.

"Are you ready to be fucked?" he asked her.

She stared deep into his eyes. "Yes." Her voice sounded breathy, stoking his need.

"I want to watch two men fucking you. Do you want both Liam and Derek to fuck you now? To feel both their big cocks inside you at the same time?"

She nodded, her eyes gleaming.

He wrapped his hand around her head and drew her face to his. Her soft lips parted and he captured her mouth, gliding his tongue inside her warmth. As her tongue danced with his, his heart ached. He loved this woman, would do anything to win her heart.

His cock, still embedded in the warmth of her sweet body, throbbed. He released her lips, barely able to stand any more of this intense intimacy without exploding inside her.

Janine stared into Sloan's blue gaze as he gently stroked her cheek. She could barely believe he had just instructed her to have sex with both Liam and Derek while he watched. He'd certainly come a long way, but . . . did she believe him? Deep inside, she was sure he was just acting the way he knew she wanted him to act to make her happy. If he was willing to go this far for her, it was impossible to deny how much she meant to him—how devoted he was to her.

She found herself lost in his adoring gaze. God, it was so clear he loved her, and that warmed her heart, at the same time as it terrified her. She did *not* want to hurt him. But she didn't want to *be* hurt, either. Not that Sloan would ever hurt her intentionally, but if they got into a deeper relationship would she eventually feel trapped? Grow to resent him? Would they wind up in a messy breakup that would destroy the closeness they now shared?

Despite the fact that she'd sought some breathing room in Kenora—and a chance to explore herself and grow as a person—she'd always wondered if someday, she'd go home to L.A. and to Sloan.

Sloan was all she had left of her brother, and if she lost Sloan, she would be totally alone. All the friends or sexual relationships in the world could not give her the same feeling of being truly loved and cherished as she'd had with Ben. And with Sloan.

But now that she and Sloan were pushing their relationship so far past their previous boundaries, she was deeply uncertain about taking such a huge risk.

She drew herself up, his gigantic cock stroking her passage as he glided free, sending quivers through her. She stood up on shaky legs and gazed at the other men. Liam smiled at her and she stepped toward him. She climbed onto his lap. He cupped her cheeks and drew her face forward. He nibbled her lower lip, then captured her mouth in a kiss. The tip of his tongue nudged at her lips and she opened, then he glided inside. She stroked his tongue as he explored her mouth. The kiss was so sweet and tender she felt her heart melt. Was it because her feelings were so raw from her encounter with Sloan, or was there something special about this man? But she'd felt it last time she'd been with him, too. Confused and uncertain, she pressed his cock to her slick opening and lowered herself onto him. His big cock didn't stretch her as much as Sloan's did, but it felt delightful gliding into her all the same. Once she was fully impaled, she leaned back and arched her breasts forward, Liam's hand flat against her back, giving her support. Derek, sitting beside Liam, stroked her breasts, then nipped one lightly. She sucked in air at the sharp pang of pleasure, thrusting her pelvis tight against Liam, driving his cock deeper. She lifted her body up and down on his cock, stroking him inside her.

Derek picked up a bottle from the side table and slathered some lubricant onto his cock until it glistened, then stood up and positioned himself behind her. Totally aware of Sloan watching her, she arched her back, raising her behind toward Derek. She felt sexy and desired.

Derek cupped her buttocks, drawing them apart, and his slick cock pressed against her opening. At the continued pressure of his cockhead pushing into her, and Liam's cock buried deep inside her, her arousal spiraled upward. She glanced toward Sloan and the intense hunger in his eyes jolted through her. Her gaze locked with his as Derek continued to fill her. The two men squeezed her tight between their bodies. She couldn't tear her gaze from Sloan's.

Derek wrapped his hands around her hips and drew her back with him, gliding Liam's cock inside her. Then Derek pushed forward. When he pulled back again, he continued farther, so his cock dragged along her back opening, stroking her insides at the same time as Liam's cock stroked her front passage. Then Derek drove forward again, driving Liam deep into her, too.

She tugged her gaze from Sloan's intense blue eyes and clung to Liam's shoulder. He smiled at her as Derek drew back again. Liam pivoted his pelvis forward, thrusting deeply into her. Derek drove forward, too, and she moaned at the intense sensation of both hard cocks filling her so fully.

The two men found a rhythm, stroking her insides as they thrust into her again and again. Intense pleasure washed through her, electrifying every cell in her body until her skin prickled with excitement. She gasped as they both drove deep again, then moaned as blissful sensations danced through her entire body. Her consciousness flared, blasting to heaven as her senses exploded in ecstasy. She wailed as the orgasm washed over her.

Both men stiffened and groaned. She could feel their cocks pulsing inside her.

She slumped against Liam's chest, her head on his shoulder. He stroked her hair back as Derek gently drew his wilted cock from her, then kissed her cheek. She breathed in deeply, relaxing against the steady thump of Liam's heart against her ear.

She opened her eyes and connected with Sloan's hot, hungry gaze.

"That was incredible to watch," Sloan said.

She couldn't stand lying there watching his hand glide up and down on his huge cock. Despite the incredible experience she'd just shared with Liam and Derek, she had a hunger for Sloan she just couldn't deny.

As she eased away from Liam, he cupped her cheek and captured her lips in a sweet, tender kiss again. She gazed into his eyes and saw a warmth that touched her heart.

Was there a chance she could find with Liam what she could never have with Sloan?

She returned his sweet kiss, then drew her lips free and stood up.

She cupped her breasts as she shifted to face Sloan.

"What would you like now, Master?"

A slow smile spread across his face. "I'm sure you know very well what I want."

He dragged her onto his lap. Her slit pressed against the length of his thick cock as he took her lips in a passionate kiss. She moved on him, gliding along his long shaft. God, she wanted him inside her.

Sensing her need, he shifted her until his cockhead pushed against her opening. She nearly fainted from pleasure as his enormous cock drove into her. He wrapped her legs around him and cupped her butt as he stood up. Their lips locked in a passionate kiss as he walked across the room, then she felt the wall against her back. Sloan drew away and thrust into her again, driving her against the wall. He kept on thrusting, like a piston filling her again and again. She clung to his shoulders and wailed as his immense cock, driving deeper and faster inside her, propelled her to incredible heights of pleasure. She clenched around him, gasping at the intensely joyful sensations throbbing through her. As he erupted inside her with a groan, she flew into ecstasy.

When she finally caught her breath again, she dropped her head against his shoulder. God, but the man could fuck her.

But more, this intimate closeness with him . . . his cock deep inside her, his arms around her, felt . . . *right*.

And that thought scared the life out of her.

"I just don't know." Janine propped her elbow on the table and leaned her chin on her hand as she stared at a woman in a canoe paddling along the river beside the café. "Why does life have to be so complicated?"

"What's complicated about it?" Derek asked.

Janine had asked him to meet her at their favorite little café along the river. They loved to come here and talk about what was going on in their lives as they watched people pass by.

"Sloan."

He raised an eyebrow. "Sloan doesn't seem too complicated to me. He's head over heels for you. That's plain to see. Don't tell me you haven't figured it out yet."

She pursed her lips. "I know. That's why I should never have agreed to get involved with him."

"Well, from what you told me about him, I wouldn't have thought your style of dating would appeal to him, but you've got to give him credit. He's coping quite well."

She banged her hand on the table. "But that's just it. I don't want a man who just 'copes' with my life. I want one who embraces it."

"What does that mean, exactly?" he asked.

She gazed at him. "Well, *you* know. You do it."

"But I'm not in love with you like Sloan is."

She sipped her white wine spritzer and gazed at the glittering river again.

"Tell me, Janine. Do you plan on getting married someday?"

"Married? Well, sure."

"And kids? The whole thing?"

Kids? She hadn't really thought about it consciously, but she knew deep inside she'd always wanted to have them.

"What are you getting at, Derek?"

"Just . . . how do you expect to meet a guy who's really serious about you, who might be interested in getting to know you well enough to actually make a lifetime commitment, if you won't give him the chance to get close? If he's constantly having to compete with other men . . . If he can never feel he's a special part of your life . . ." Derek shrugged.

"I think the right guy won't be intimidated by other men. He'll get to know me and we'll move it to the next level."

"How?"

She shrugged. "I don't know. It'll just happen."

"And what is the next level? Does that mean you'll make a commitment to that one man and drop the others?"

Her hand wrapped around her glass as she shifted in her chair. "I don't know, exactly. I guess I'll figure that out when the time comes."

"Don't look now, but I think the time has come. Sloan is definitely ready to move to that next level you're talking about, whatever that is, exactly." Derek leaned toward her. "Are you in love with him?"

She shook her head. "It doesn't matter. Love isn't enough." Her fingers clenched around her glass. "Love shouldn't require a person to be someone they're not. I have to be who I am, and I can't change for Sloan."

It wasn't just about her sex life. It was about her being a free spirit who liked to push the limits. She couldn't live in a safe little box like Sloan would have her do. To live within other people's constraining views of the world.

"That's true. You do have to be who you are. I'm not denying that."

She gazed at Derek in frustration. "Why does the world expect a woman to commit to just one man to find happiness?" She sipped her wine, then frowned. "And why can't I be satisfied with one person when the rest of the world is

perfectly happy that way? Why can't I be satisfied with normal, everyday sex? It would sure make life a lot easier."

He shrugged. "That's traditional thinking, but you're not
traditional. You don't have to follow other people's rules. You
just need to stay true to yourself and make sure you're with a
man who's compatible."

She rested her cheek on her hand. "I just want to find a
way that Sloan and I can both be happy. Unfortunately, I don't
think we can do that together."

Fifteen

Janine glanced in her rearview mirror. A squad car followed her with its lights flashing. She pulled onto the shoulder to let him pass.

Damn! He pulled in behind her.

She grabbed her purse from the passenger seat and pulled out her wallet, then fumbled for her license. She could see the officer walking along the shoulder toward her car. She pressed the button to lower her window as he approached her door, then handed him her license.

"Good evening, Officer"—she glanced at his badge to see his name—"O'Neill. Did I do something wrong?"

"Janine?"

She glanced up to see Liam staring down at her with a grin. She hadn't even thought about the fact she didn't know his last name.

"Officer Liam." Oh, God, she was an idiot. She sucked in a breath. "I mean . . . Liam. Is it okay if I call you Liam, with you in uniform and all?" Oh, God. A real idiot.

He chuckled. "Relax. I only pulled you over because your license plate sticker is out of date."

"Oh, but . . . I bought it last month."

"It's not on your plate."

She stared at him blankly. She'd definitely gone into the DMV and picked it up, then brought it out to the car and put it in the glove compartment, then . . . Oh, damn, forgotten all about it.

"It's in my glove compartment."

"It's not doing you much good in there now, is it?"

Her gaze lurched to his. He was grinning at her. She relaxed a little, her shoulders lowering and her jaw unclenching.

"Do you have to give me a ticket?"

"No, just a reminder to actually stick it on your plate." He leaned a little closer, as if looking into her car. "Janine, really, relax. It's just me."

"You in uniform."

He gazed at her with a gleam in his eyes. "Does the uniform intimidate you?"

"Um . . ." She stared at his twinkling eyes and laughed. "Yeah, I guess. A little bit."

His smile broadened. "Does it turn you on?"

Excitement flashed through her as she thought of him snapping handcuffs onto her wrists, and she sucked in air.

"Um . . . actually"—she smiled up at him, hunger growing inside her—"it does."

Heat filled his eyes. "I've just finished my shift. Would you like to grab a coffee somewhere? I could meet you in about a half hour."

She knew Sloan would not be happy if she had a date with

Liam, but she had warned Sloan that she wouldn't be exclusive. She couldn't let his expectations change her.

"Will you still be"—she smiled enticingly—"in uniform?"

"I could be."

"And . . . will you have your handcuffs with you?"

His eyes lit up. "Absolutely."

"Then why don't we go back to my place for coffee?"

He smiled. "That sounds like a great idea."

"Thank you, Officer O'Neill. I assume you have my address?"

He handed back her license. "Yes, Miss Reid, I do. A half hour, then."

He turned and walked back to his squad car. She felt totally wicked as she watched his tight, uniformed butt in her mirror. But oh, man, he was sooo sexy in uniform.

Her insides quivered as she put her car in gear and pulled back into the traffic, knowing the half-hour wait would feel like an eternity.

Janine's buzzer sounded and she raced to the intercom and pushed the button. "Yes?"

"Ma'am, it's Officer O'Neill here. May I come up?"

A shiver danced along her spine. "Of course, Officer." She pushed the button to unlock the outside door.

Many long minutes later, a knock sounded at her door. She peered through the peephole and there stood Liam in his blue uniform, right down to the hat. She pulled open the door.

"Yes, Officer. May I help you?"

"May I come in, ma'am?"

God, he was so sexy and . . . a little intimidating with authoritative air. "Of course." She stepped back so he could step inside. His muscular arm brushed hers as he went past and heat washed through her.

He closed the door behind him, glancing around her apartment.

"Nice place, ma'am."

She turned to face him. "What's this all about, Officer?"

"I'm sorry, ma'am, but I'm here to place you under arrest." He opened a leather pouch on his belt and pulled out a pair of silver handcuffs.

He took her right wrist and snapped a cold cuff around it, then drew her arm behind her, captured her other wrist, and cuffed it, too. Excitement quivered through her.

"But why?"

"For wielding a dangerous weapon."

She turned to face him, her hands trapped firmly behind her back. "What weapon?"

He grinned. "Well, basically, a killer body."

His gaze traveled to her breasts, which were thrust forward because her hands were behind her back, and lingered long enough that her nipples throbbed with need.

"Are you going to take me to jail?"

"Yes, ma'am, but first I'd better search you."

He turned her around and took her arm, then guided her into the kitchen.

"Stand facing the counter."

She shivered at the authority in his voice. She turned around and faced the counter that overlooked her eating area and the sliding door to the balcony. He stepped close behind her.

"Spread your legs, ma'am."

She almost gasped at the thrill of adrenaline rushing through her. She shifted her feet apart. His hand flattened on her back and he pressed her forward and down, until her upper body rested on the cold marble. He placed his hands on her head, glided downward through her hair, along her neck, then across her shoulders. His thumbs stroked firmly down her back while his fingers grazed her sides, then continued down her hips and over her ass. He patted her round flesh thoroughly, then continued down her legs.

Once he reached her ankles, he continued back up, following her inner legs. When he reached the bottom of her skirt, his hands moved away and she felt the button on the back of her skirt release, then the zipper open. He drew her skirt down her hips and off.

His hands brushed her legs again, starting at her knees, then gliding up her inner thighs. He toyed with the lace edge of her elastic-topped stockings, which she'd put on as soon as she got home, then continued upward. Her breath caught as he brushed against the silky crotch of her panties, then over her ass, which was essentially naked since she wore a thong. He cupped her cheeks and squeezed enticingly.

"Stand up, ma'am."

She stood up. He stepped closer, his body pressed against her back, the bulge in his pants pushing into her hands, which were still cuffed behind her back, palms toward him. She could feel the hardness of his shaft. His hands glided around her waist, then upward. He cupped her breasts and squeezed, pulling her tight to his body. She could feel his breath on her ear. Then one hand slid downward and stroked along the crotch of her panties, which had to be totally wet because the way he was touching her. His body pressed against hers, his erection in her hands, made her melt inside.

"Sorry, ma'am," he murmured against her ear, his voice a little raspy, "but this is definitely a killer body." He cupped her mound and tightened his fingers. "You are in some trouble."

She pressed her hands tighter against his growing bulge. "But, Officer, is there anything I can do to get out of trouble?"

He turned her around, then pressed her against the counter, his pelvis tight to hers. Her breath caught at being pinned to the counter in such an intimate way by this tall, devastatingly handsome, uniformed man. "That wouldn't be fair. Letting you go unpunished for your crime."

She sent him a sultry gaze. "I didn't say you shouldn't *punish* me."

He arched an eyebrow. "Really? What do you have in mind?"

"Well, you could always spank me."

He smiled, then turned her around again and leaned her over the counter.

"Your delightful ass looks like it could use a good spanking." A loud smack sounded as his palm connected with her skin. He smacked again and her flesh stung delightfully.

He smacked the other cheek, then caressed over her round, undoubtedly pink flesh. Then his hand connected again, followed by another caress.

"I don't think a spanking is enough to teach you a lesson." He drew her from the counter and unfastened one wrist, then the other from the handcuffs. "Why don't you show me how you use your killer body to entice men."

She smiled and stroked her hand down the placket of her blouse, then unfastened the top button. "Of course, Officer."

She released each button in turn until the blouse draped open, then drew back the fabric briefly, giving him a glimpse of her black lace bra before she grasped the fabric closed at the front. She dropped her blouse off one shoulder, then the other, then caressed her breasts through the fabric. Doing this in front of him while he stood there in full uniform watching her sent a tremor through her. She stroked down the front of her blouse, then dropped it off her arms and let it fall to the floor.

Now she stood before him in only her black lace bra, panties, and garterless black stockings. She stroked her breasts, then pressed them together, forcing them to swell over her bra cups. His olive green eyes darkened. She reached behind her back, thrusting her breasts forward, and unfastened her bra, then dropped the straps from her shoulders. Slowly, she lowered the bra a little until one nipple peeked out. His gaze burned into her. She lowered the other side, revealing the other nipple. Both poked forward, hard and needy. She dropped the bra and stroked over her hard nipples, enjoying the heat tingling through her, then cupped under her breasts and lifted. Her thumbs stroked over her hard buds.

"My nipples are very hard. Would you like to feel them?" she asked.

He took off his hat and tossed it on the counter, then reached toward her and ran his hand over her breast. His fingertips found her aching nipple and she sucked in air as he stroked, then squeezed.

"You're right. They're very hard."

He leaned forward and licked one nub, then drew it into his mouth. When he sucked, she gasped at the intense pleasure. His hand found her other nipple and he stroked it as he sucked the first. A moment later he drew back, but his gaze

171

remained on her breasts. He moved to the kitchen table and sat down in one of the chairs.

"Very good, ma'am. Now I'd like to see more."

She smiled. "Of course, Officer."

She glided her hands over her breasts again, wishing they were his hands—or better, his mouth—caressing her right now. She stroked down her stomach, then glided her fingers over the crotch of her panties. His cock stirred beneath his uniform pants. She slid her hand under the fabric and caressed her intimate folds, feeling the slickness.

"Mmm. It's very wet." She walked toward him and pulled the fabric of her crotch forward. "Would you like to feel?"

Liam's gaze dropped to her exposed pussy. Damn, but this woman was hot. This role-playing was driving him insane with need. He wanted to run his hands all over her, then drive his cock home.

He pressed his hand to her flat stomach, then moved downward, under the fabric. The moment his fingers touched her slit, he could feel the hot slickness. He grasped her hip and turned her around.

"Sit on my lap." His voice came out husky.

She sat down and he slid his fingers inside her panties and glided along her dripping pussy. With his free hand, he cupped her luscious breast and his thumb stroked over her tight nipple. He hooked a finger and slid it into her slick passage. His thumb found her clit and he stroked it. Her breathing accelerated.

"You like that?"

She sucked in air and nodded. He glided his finger deeper into her while at the same time flicking her clit. Her body trembled against him. She was close. He flicked one more time, then stopped. She moaned in frustration.

"This seems more like a reward than a punishment," he said.

She stood up and turned around, then knelt in front of him.

"I have an idea." She stroked his aching cock, then released his belt and lowered his zipper. Her hand slipped into his pants and stroked his cock through the thin cotton of his boxers. The moment her hand slipped under the fabric and stroked his hard flesh, he groaned.

Janine wrapped her hand around his thick cock and stroked. He was longer than Jonas, but not quite as long as Derek—and nowhere close to Sloan, but who was? He was thicker than Derek and didn't have the distinct veins along his shaft. The feel of his kid-leather-soft skin in her hand as it glided over the rigid shaft sent a quiver down her spine.

He was incredibly hard. She would love to feel him slide into her right now. She drew him out of the boxers and stroked his long shaft, then leaned forward and kissed the tip of him. She swirled her tongue over his cockhead, then spiraled around.

"Do you like that, Officer?"

"Oh, yeah."

Janine smiled, then swallowed his cockhead into her mouth. Dragging her tongue around the underside of the corona caused Liam to gasp. She squeezed him in her mouth, then dove down deep, taking all of him in her mouth. He groaned as she glided up and down, squeezing him, then sucking, then squeezing again. She tucked her hand under his cock and cupped his balls, then kneaded gently.

His balls tightened and he sucked in air.

"Ma'am, stop. Now."

She released his cock and gazed up at him. He sucked in air, clearly trying to calm himself. She backed toward the counter, stroking her hand over her crotch, then glided her hand inside her panties to stroke her wet slit again. She drew her hand out and stroked over the fabric, then tightened her hand around it and tugged it tight, pulling the fabric into her slit as she rocked her pelvis forward and back. She spun around and leaned against the counter, giving him a great view of her ass, then glided the thong down her hips and pushed it down her legs. She kicked it aside and climbed onto the countertop on her hands and knees. She arched forward, dragging her nipples along the cold marble, then lifted her shoulders a little, giving him a view of her breasts pointing toward the black marble counter. She pivoted around to face him, then pushed up onto her knees and stroked her bare breasts, tweaking the nipples. Her other hand stroked between her legs, over her slit.

Liam stood up and walked toward her, his eyes glazed with need. He cupped his hands over her breasts and stroked, then grasped one in his mouth, sucking deeply. She moaned as pleasure spiked through her. Then he stroked down to her stomach and over her folds. He opened her with his thumbs, then leaned forward and licked her slit. Pleasure spiraled through her. He found her clit and licked it, then sucked. She moaned at the sharp pang of pleasure.

He grasped her waist with both hands and drew her forward.

"Sit," he commanded.

She dropped her ass to the cold counter and draped her legs over the side. He stepped between her thighs, his hand wrapped around his big, hard cock. He pressed it to her wet folds, then thrust deep into her.

"Oh, God, yes." Intense pleasure vaulted through her at his sudden invasion. She wrapped her arms around him and held him tight. "Fuck me, Officer. Keep driving your big cock into me. Hard."

He drew back and thrust again. She moaned.

"God damn. You are so fucking hot." He drove deep again, his big cock gliding along her slick passage.

"Oh . . . keep doing that, Officer O'Neill. You're going to make me come."

"Oh, fuck." He drove deep again, his forceful thrust filling her with exquisite pleasure.

She clung to his shoulders and whimpered in need. "Faster, Officer . . . Please make me come."

Janine squeezed his big cock inside her as he drew back, intensifying the feel of his corona dragging against her sensitive passage. When he thrust forward again, she gasped. Pleasure pummeled her insides, then shot through her entire body. She gasped as she plummeted into ecstasy.

Still he kept pumping into her.

"Are you coming?" he murmured against her ear.

She nodded.

"Tell me," he demanded.

"I'm . . ." She gasped. "Ohhh . . . I'm . . . coming." She wailed as the blissful pleasure exploded.

He groaned, still driving his hard shaft deep inside her.

Again and again. Then he spiked forward, holding her tight against his body, his pelvis grinding against her, and his whole body shuddered.

She stroked his short, sandy hair as she sucked in air, finally catching her breath, then nuzzled his ear.

"Officer, did I convince you not to send me to jail?"

Liam drew back and gazed at her, then captured her mouth in a stunning kiss. His lips moved on hers with quiet authority, his tongue driving into her mouth with determination. His cock, still inside her, twitched and swelled. He glided his tongue around the inside of her mouth, then drew back, leaving her gasping for breath.

"I don't know. I'll have to sleep on it."

Then he lifted her off the counter, took her hand, and led her to the bedroom.

Sixteen

Janine opened her eyes to see a blue uniform draped over the armchair beside her bed. Liam's arms were tucked around her waist, holding her snug against his solid, muscular body.

Aw, damn, Sloan would have a fit if he knew Liam had spent the night with her. But she couldn't let thoughts of what Sloan wanted control her.

She felt his lips move against the back of her neck, nuzzling, kissing.

She smiled and turned to face him. She pressed her hand flat against his muscle-ridged chest and dragged her hand downward, over his well-defined abs, then wrapped her hands around his swelling cock.

"Good morning, Officer." As she stroked his cock, it grew harder.

He grabbed her hand and rolled her onto her back, pinning both her hands beside her head.

"Good morning." He lowered his mouth to hers and kissed her, gliding his tongue into her mouth. "How's my prisoner this morning?"

Her insides quivered. She attempted to come up with a coy answer, but he captured her mouth again, driving his tongue deep, leaving her breathless. He nuzzled her neck, sending tingles through her, then kissed down her chest. When he licked her nipple, then sucked, she arched against him, her hands still held firmly in his grasp.

He released her wrists, and cupped her breasts, then pressed them together. His lips traveled over her mounds, nuzzling and kissing. Then he found her other nipple and sucked. She forked her fingers through his short, sandy hair, and gasped as he nipped her nub lightly with his teeth.

"I'm still considering whether to let you go or not. Show me again how sexy you can be." He pushed himself up and sat beside her hip, watching her.

She smiled and dragged her hands over her breasts, stroking their undersides, then moving over her nipples. She squeezed the tight nubs between her fingertips, then caressed her breasts again, watching Liam's olive green eyes darken.

Her hand glided down her stomach, over her pubic hair, and covered her mound. He watched, his eyes glimmering with need.

She dragged a finger over her slit, back and forth, then slid one finger inside her slick passage.

"Oh, man, that is so sexy."

She widened her legs to give him a better view, then bent her knees and arched her hips upward. He glided his hand down her stomach, then over her hand. His finger slid inside her, joining hers.

"Do you like that?" he asked.

Was he kidding? It felt incredible.

She nodded, arching upward again. He drew his finger

free, then slid his arms around her and cupped her ass. His lips trailed along her arm, down to her busy hand, then he nibbled the knuckle of the finger inside her. She slid it free and he grasped her wrist, then drew her damp finger into his mouth. He sucked for a few seconds, then drew it from his lips.

"I didn't tell you to take it out." He guided her hand back to her slit and she slid her finger inside again.

He kissed her hand, then licked her slit. His tongue curled around her finger, teasing it, and he nibbled her folds. Finally, he drew her hand away and licked the length of her opening.

"Now show me how you touch your clit," he said.

She pressed her finger into her folds, then found the little button hidden inside. She stroked it lightly, then dabbed.

"Show me your clit," he said.

Liam stared at her wet folds of flesh as she parted them with her fingers, revealing a little nub of flesh inside. God, this woman was something else. So open and comfortable with her body and sex. Willing to be wild and totally uninhibited.

He leaned forward and licked her glistening clit. Tingles rushed through him when she moaned. If he kept working on her clit, licking it . . . sucking it . . . she would come. And he wanted to see her come again. But in the state he was in, if he made her come now, he'd spew all over her at the same time, and he'd rather be inside her.

He glided upward and grabbed her hands, then pinned her to the bed again, holding her body trapped beneath his.

"I'm going to fuck you now." He nipped her lower lip. "I'm going to drive my cock into you so deep and so hard, you'll beg me for more."

"Oh, yes."

He locked his gaze on her glazed blue eyes as he pressed his cockhead to her wet opening, wondering if he'd make it inside her. He thrust forward—deep, just like he'd promised—into her hot depths. Her hot, wet sheath tightened around him as she squeezed. He groaned at the intense sensation. He drew back, then glided forward again. His lips found the soft skin of her neck and he nuzzled. She gazed up at him and he captured her lips as he drove into her again.

He drew back, then paused, watching with a smile as her expression grew more needy.

She squeezed him again and moaned. "Don't stop."

"If you want me to keep going, you know what you have to do."

Her gaze caught his and she smiled. "Oh, Officer, please. I'm so close to coming. Please fuck me."

"You're close?" He drove in deep, then held her pinned to the bed.

Her deep, rapid breathing gave him a pretty good clue.

"I'm sooo close. Please keep fucking me."

He drew back and drove deep again, then again, picking up speed until he was hammering into her.

"Oh, God. Oh, yes." Her hands glided over his shoulders and she began to wail. "More. Yes." Her fingers tightened. "Oh, yes. I'm . . . ah . . . coming."

As soon as she said the words, heat flooded through his groin. As he drove deep again, he erupted inside her, groaning at the exquisite release.

Still he thrust into her. Her orgasm seemed to last forever, as she moaned and clutched him tight.

Her moans turned to whimpers, and finally she collapsed

onto the bed and pushed her long, blond hair from her face. She smiled up at him.

"Officer, if I haven't convinced you yet to set me free, I'm not sure what else to do."

In fact, he wondered if he ever wanted to set her free.

He'd never met a woman like Janine, who was so comfortable just being herself, not caring what society or others thought about how she lived her life. He loved that about her. In fact, maybe he was actually falling in love with this woman.

"Well, I'm not sure I'm totally convinced. Maybe I'll need to keep an eye on you for a while. At least for the rest of the day." He kissed her soundly, loving the feel of her soft lips against his.

"Of course, Officer. Whatever you say."

A knock sounded at the door and Janine glanced up from her computer. That was probably Liam. He had called about an hour ago to ask if he'd left his sunglasses behind the other day. She'd found them on the kitchen counter and he'd said he might drop by to pick them up.

A big smile claimed her face as she remembered the wonderful day they'd spent together. He was so easy to be with . . . and so intensely sexy. She hurried to the door and pulled it open, looking forward to seeing him again.

"Sloan."

"Don't look so disappointed."

"No, I'm not. I just . . . was expecting a friend to stop by."

"You have plans?" He held up an aromatic brown paper bag. "I was hoping you were free for dinner. I brought your favorite. Moo Shoo pork."

"Oh, well, come in." She stepped back and he stepped past her and walked to the dining room.

She closed the door as he set the bag of food on the dining table. He headed into the kitchen and she heard him gather plates and cutlery. She glanced at the table near the door and noticed Liam's sunglasses. She snatched them up and stuffed them into the drawer in the front of the table, a pang of guilt slicing through her at seeing Liam behind Sloan's back.

But it wasn't behind his back, damn it.

She should talk to Sloan. Letting him go on believing there was a chance for a real relationship—as he defined relationships, anyway—wasn't fair to him. She'd have a nice dinner with him, and then they'd talk.

She glanced at the door. But what if Liam showed up? It would be awkward and might even cause a big fight, which would totally defocus the real discussion she should be having with Sloan. Maybe she should call Liam.

She heard a clatter and glanced around to see Sloan placing the plates and cutlery on the table. He set them out neatly.

"Do you have a friend coming over?" he asked.

"Friend?"

"Yes. You mentioned that you were expecting a friend."

"Oh, yes. Well, just someone who might drop by to pick something up but . . ." She glanced at him. "You really should have called. I do have a life, you know."

He smiled and stepped toward her. "I know that. But it wouldn't have been much of a surprise if I announced it ahead of time now, would it?"

He wrapped his arm around her and dragged her against his body, then captured her lips with his firm mouth. His tongue dipped inside her and swirled around. She wrapped her arms around his neck, hanging on for support at the sensual onslaught.

Then their lips parted and he gazed down at her with a smile.

"Anyway, I really wanted to see you. I've missed you."

She glanced at the bag of food on the table, still clinging to him while she caught her breath from the sensational kiss.

"It does smell good, but . . ."

"But? I don't like the sound of that."

The buzzer by the door sounded. Someone at the lobby door for her. Probably Liam.

Oh, God, she did not want to have Liam come up right now. It wasn't just awkwardness she was avoiding. She didn't want to hurt Sloan. She'd tell him about Liam—it wasn't her intention to be dishonest—but she'd do it gently.

"That must be your friend." Sloan released her, but she tugged him close again and kissed him soundly.

Butterflies fluttered in her stomach as his hand stroked down her back, then cupped her butt as he pulled her tight to him against a very hard bulge in his pants.

"*But,*" she continued, "I have something in mind besides eating right now."

The buzzer sounded again. He grinned. "So your friend be damned?"

She nodded, then leaned in for another kiss. His skillful lips moved against hers hungrily and her heart quivered. She *wanted* to be with Sloan right now. She felt bad about leaving Liam hanging, but it hadn't been definite that she'd be here. He'd understand.

She turned Sloan and backed him up against the wall, then ground her pelvis against his growing erection. She stroked down his chest, then over his bulge.

"It seems you have another little surprise for me," she said.

"Well, it's not really a surprise . . . and I guarantee you, it's not little."

She laughed and sank to her knees in front of him.

"Let's see." She slid his zipper down and reached inside. Her hand wrapped around hot, hard flesh and she drew out his shaft.

"You're right. Nothing small about this." She gazed at his humongous cock and grinned, then wrapped her mouth around his large cockhead. She swirled her tongue over his hard flesh as his fingers forked through her long hair.

"Oh, God, Janine. You do that so well."

She tugged his jeans down as she sucked and squeezed him, then tucked her hand under his balls. She slid her mouth off him and glided her hand up and down his slick shaft.

"You are deliciously huge and I can hardly wait to feel you inside me."

"God, Janine, the way you talk."

She gazed up at him. "You don't like it?"

"Are you kidding? I love it."

She laughed and licked down his shaft, then over his shaven balls. She laved them again and again, then took one in her mouth.

A knock sounded at the door.

"Your friend"—Sloan sucked in a breath as she squeezed his sack in her mouth—"is persistent."

Damn. Liam must have slipped in when another tenant came in.

She drew back her face, but kept stroking his cock. "You want me to answer it?"

God, please say "no."

"No way."

A knock sounded again. She swallowed Sloan and sucked earnestly. Sloan leaned against the wall, his hand stroking her head. His breathing accelerated.

She fondled his balls as she moved up and down on his cock. He groaned and stiffened. She squeezed his cock in her mouth, then dove down deep, taking most of him inside.

He groaned again, and hot liquid filled her throat. She wrapped her hand around his tight butt and squeezed as she swallowed.

Once he was finished, she released him and he grabbed her and dragged her to her feet. Then he spun her around and pressed her against the wall, almost tripping on the jeans around his ankles. His lips pressed hard against hers and his tongue drove into her and swirled inside until he left her breathless. He fished in his denim jacket pocket.

"You are a very bad girl, making our dinner get cold."

She felt cold metal against her wrist and heard the sound of a metal cuff snapping closed. He took her other hand and dragged her down the hall, then into her bedroom. He sat her on the bed, flattened a hand on her chest and pressed her onto her back, then slid her to the middle of the bed. Finally he hooked the chain of the handcuffs around a bar of her headboard and clasped the other bracelet around her free wrist.

She lay there, blinking at him, her heart thundering in her chest. It had happened fast. A moment ago, she'd been standing in the entrance sucking his cock, now she was flat on her back, handcuffed.

Opal Carew

And she had on too many damned clothes.

Sloan stripped off his jacket and shirt, then tossed his boxers aside. Totally naked, he climbed onto the bed and knelt over her, a knee on either side of her thighs. He stroked down the front of her T-shirt and over her hips. His hands glided over her stomach, then down her crotch. Damn, the jeans she wore were in the way. But his fingers glided over her crotch back and forth. Driving her wild.

He chuckled, then slid his hands up again, this time underneath her T-shirt, and cupped her breasts. The nipples rose shamelessly, peaking into his palms. He rolled her T-shirt up, then reached under her and unclasped her bra. His hands slid under the cups and he teased her sensitive nipples until she cried out in pleasure. He pushed the bra up out of the way.

"You have the most beautiful breasts." He gazed at them in awe, then leaned down and took one nipple in his mouth.

He teased the tip with his tongue, then sucked. She arched forward and gasped. While still sucking on her, he slid his other hand down her belly, then unfastened her jeans button and zipper. His hand stole into her jeans, then under her panties, and he stroked her damp slit.

"Oh, yes."

His finger slipped inside her. He switched to her other nipple and tortured that one with his tongue, then sucked. Intense sensations sparked through her. She arched her hips against his hand, driving his finger deeper. His finger slipped from inside her and he drew back, then tugged her jeans down her hips. He tossed them aside and stripped off her panties.

As he gazed at her folds, she glanced down to his swollen cock. God, she wanted that monster driving inside her.

"Mr. Policeman, are you going to drive that big nightstick of yours into me?"

He wrapped his hand around his enormous cock. "You mean this?"

She nodded, her eyes wide.

He stroked it, then tapped the hot, hard flesh against her belly.

"It sounds like you'd like me to."

"Oh, no, I don't want to be pounded with your big . . . stick."

He chuckled. "That's good. Because it wouldn't be a punishment then, would it?"

To her surprise, he grabbed her hip and turned her onto her side, then slid in behind her. His hard cock brushed against her ass, then she felt the length of the shaft press between her cheeks. His arm came around her and he stroked her breasts, back and forth with one hand, teasing the tight buds until they wanted to burst. Then his cock glided down, and he pushed it between her legs. His cockhead nudged her slick slit and the head pushed into her. Suddenly, he thrust inside and she gasped in pleasure.

His huge cock so deep inside her, plunging in so suddenly, sent stars flashing through her head. He held her tight against his body, one hand cupping her breast, the other flat on her stomach.

"Are you ready for your punishment?" he murmured against her ear.

"Oh, yes . . . I mean . . . no."

He chuckled again. His finger found her clit and he toyed with it, sending jolting sparks of pleasure through her as he drew his long cock down her passage. Then he thrust back inside. She gasped again. His finger teased her sensitive bud as he pulled back and thrust forward again.

God, she was close.

Her breathing accelerated as he thrust again and again until she could hardly catch her breath. He rammed inside her, filling her with his thick, hard shaft. Harder. Filling her impossibly full each time.

She gasped as pleasure burst through her, then wailed as she catapulted to a joyous orgasm, waves of ecstasy washing over her.

Sloan groaned and erupted inside her.

She squeezed and moaned as her orgasm went on and on.

Finally, she slumped back against his solid chest.

He kissed the back of her neck.

"Have you learned your lesson?" he asked.

"Mmm." She lolled her head against his muscular shoulder and gazed around at him. "I'm not sure."

He drove deep into her and pleasure blasted through her again. He pumped a few more times, teasing her clit at the same time, sending her trembling into another orgasm.

She caught her breath and laughed giddily. "Well, maybe I have learned something."

He laughed and stroked her breasts, then she felt his cock withdraw. He rolled her onto her back and prowled over her, then kissed her. Sweet and passionate. Her heart swelled and she melted into the kiss. When he released her mouth, she gazed up at him . . . and saw love in his eyes. Pure, unadulterated love.

Oh, God, what have I done?

Seventeen

Sloan watched Janine's expression grow guarded as he gazed down at her. What had happened to throw up her barriers?

"Sloan, what are we doing?" Janine asked.

He kissed her shoulder and rolled onto his side. "Well, I think we're basking in afterglow."

"I mean this. You and me. We want different things from a relationship."

Damn, he didn't like the sound of this.

"All I want is you."

"No, you don't. You want a woman who will be true to you. Who wants to be with you alone."

He sat up. "What's wrong with that?"

"That's not me, that's what."

"It could be if you'd give it a chance."

She waved her finger at him. "That's the problem right there. You believe I just have to fall in love with you and I'll give up my wanton ways to be with you."

"I didn't say your ways were wanton."

"No, but you have been hoping I'll fall madly in love with you and want to be with you exclusively. Admit it."

He crossed his legs and gazed down at her. "Okay, I really do believe you have feelings for me. That if you'd just let yourself, you'd fall in love with me."

She pushed herself up on one elbow and stared at him with earnest blue eyes. "That's the thing. I am in love with you."

He stared at her and blinked.

"You're in love with me?" His heart wanted to soar, but caution gripped him.

"I've known I loved you since that first kiss years ago," she continued. "But I knew it wouldn't work then and I know it won't work now."

"But . . . *why not*?"

"Face it, Sloan. We want different things. But mostly, you want me to change, and I can't change for you. Neither of us would ever be happy."

"Try me."

"Sloan, we need to end this now, before either of us gets hurt."

When he gazed into her eyes, he saw the pain there and realized he wasn't the only one fighting for what he wanted. She wanted him, too, but she couldn't give up herself to have him.

His chest compressed. And he shouldn't expect her to.

Damn it, what the hell was wrong with him? She had to be who she was, not who he wanted her to be, otherwise she could never be truly happy. And neither would he.

"Okay, you're right. I have been hoping you'd choose to give up seeing other guys and just be with me. I love you.

What else could you expect? But I understand that you need to be who you are. I respect that."

He took her hand. "Give me another chance to prove that I do accept you for who you are . . . and I'll give you all the space you need."

Janine wasn't quite sure what to expect when she walked down the steps to the dungeon area of the cabin they'd rented for this weekend fantasy. A dungeon-and-breakfast. She'd never heard of such a thing before. Sloan certainly was getting good at being a little kinky.

Sloan had told her she'd be serving in a bar, but he hadn't explained how she'd be serving. Was she to be a barmaid? A love slave? A stripper doing lap dances?

At the bottom of the steps she found a hallway. In front of her was a door with a sheet of white paper taped to it. The word BAR was written in bold black letters. She opened the door, then stepped into a softly lit room with two round tables like you'd find in a café, a bar at the end, a stripper pole in the center and . . . four cops in uniform. Her knees felt weak as she glanced around at Jonas, Derek, Liam and Sloan in full uniform, hats and all, sitting at the two tables talking.

"Ah, there's our waitress," Sloan said, and all the men turned to stare at her.

"Waitress, bring us beers all around," Jonas said.

She smiled. "Of course."

She walked to the bar and opened the small fridge under the counter. All she could find were cans of root beer. She pulled out four cans and placed them on the counter. Next to an insulated bucket were four tall glasses on a round brown tray. She filled each glass with ice, then opened each can and poured it into a glass to the sound of cracking ice and fizz.

She carried the tray to one of the tables and raised an eyebrow. "Root beer?"

"Yes, ma'am," Liam said. "We're on duty."

"I see." She set a glass in front of each of them.

Sloan tossed a couple of bills on the tray, with a slip of white paper between them. She took the bills, pretending not to notice the paper, and slid them into her neckline, then stowed them in her bra cup. When she returned to the bar to set down the tray, she pulled out the note.

Go to the staff room.

She glanced across the room and noticed a white piece of paper taped to a door with the words STAFF ONLY written on it. She crossed to the door and stepped inside. A large bed with a big wooden headboard dominated the room. Around the room were various pieces of equipment. A St. Andrew's cross stood in the corner, chains near the ends of the X for attaching wrists and ankles. On the other side of the room was a spanking bench with padded knee and chest rests. There was even a suspension hook on the ceiling and an array of floggers, whips, and crops along one wall.

On the bed was a note and a small overnight bag. She walked to the bed and read the note.

Put on the outfit in the bag, then return to the bar.

She unzipped the case. On top lay a short leather jacket and a pair of thigh-high, spike-heeled boots. She picked up the boots and set them on the bed, then the jacket. Underneath, she found a short black leather skirt with a silver zipper down the front edged with silver studs, and a sexy bra and thong in black lace with red lining. She slipped off her clothes and put on the bra and thong and glanced at herself in the mirror. The thong was basically a three-inch-wide lace band around her hips with a tiny bit of fabric covering her crotch. She put on the short skirt, then sat down and pulled on one of the boots and tugged the zipper tag to the top at mid-thigh, an inch below the hem of the skirt. She pulled on the other boot and zipped it up, then stood, grabbing the jacket and tugging it on. She gazed in the mirror, turning from side to side. Anticipation quivered through her as she thought of returning to the room with the four uniformed men.

She zipped up the jacket just enough to cover the bra, then walked to the door.

She opened it and walked across the room, then stood behind the bar. None of the men even glanced in her direction. They just talked and drank their root beers.

A moment later, the lights dimmed and an overhead light turned on, casting light on the pole. Then music began to play. One of the men must have started it with a remote control. The lights, too.

It was deep, jazzy strip music. Obviously, her cue.

She sauntered to the pole and smiled at the men. They watched her, keeping their expressions serious. She swayed her body to the music and unzipped her jacket slowly, then lowered the jacket over one shoulder then the other. Then she drew open the jacket to reveal her sexy bra. Leaving the jacket draped low on her shoulders, she unfastened the zipper down the front of her skirt and tossed it aside. She turned around and swayed her behind back and forth. When she turned around again, all four pairs of eyes stared at her with tremendous heat, despite the men's carefully maintained, reserved expressions.

She smiled and allowed her jacket to drop off one arm, then the other, and she kicked it away. Grabbing the pole, she spun around, then stopped behind it, facing them. She arched toward the pole and stroked it lovingly, giving them an idea what she'd love to do to their swelling poles right now. Her lips met the cold, hard metal and she wrapped her hands around it and kissed it, then ran her tongue along it.

Jonas shifted in his seat and Derek's gaze lingered on the swell of her breasts. She hooked her leg around the pole and drew her body close to it, then arched her pelvis against it. Liam watched her lower body as she pivoted forward and back against the pole. Sloan took a sip of his root beer, his gaze gliding up and down her body.

Her nipples hardened and her insides tightened at the anticipation of being touched and caressed very soon by these sexy, hunky men in uniform. She turned her body around the pole until her back was to them, then released the pole and reached behind her. A quick flick unhooked her bra and she glided the garment from her body and tossed it over her shoulder. She turned back, her hands covering her aching breasts. All eyes were on her hands as she squeezed her breasts together, then slowly glided away, finally baring them to view.

Derek licked his lips. Liam's hand tightened around his glass. She stroked down her torso, then over her panties. She caressed the fabric, sliding her hand over her mound, up and down. She could feel the tension in the men, especially as they tried to keep their expressions solemn. She dipped her hand under the fabric and stroked her damp slit. God, she was hot for them. She could hardly wait to feel their hands on her, to feel their cocks inside her.

She glided her damp hand upward and pulled at the elastic, then hooked her other hand under the elastic, too, and drew it away from her body, teasing them. She turned around and pushed the thong downward, over her thigh-high boots to her ankles, then tipped one foot forward, lifting the heel from the floor.

"Freeze, ma'am," Liam said.

At his words, she stopped moving, her naked butt high in the air, one knee bent forward and her fingers interrupted in the process of pushing the lacy thong over the high heel. She glanced between her ankles to see the upside-down forms of the uniformed men move toward her. One grasped her arm and drew her to her feet.

"What's going on?" she asked.

"Ma'am, you have just broken the law. This establishment is licensed for topless dancing only. Full nudity is not allowed."

"I'm sorry, Officers. I didn't know."

"That's no excuse, ma'am."

"Lift your foot, ma'am," Jonas said. When she did, he drew the thong over the boot heel and off her toe. "Now the other one." He pulled the thong all the way off, then tucked it in his pocket.

Locking gazes with her, he nodded. "Evidence."

Derek clamped a metal cuff around one wrist, snapped the cuff closed, then drew her wrist behind her back and cuffed the other wrist. He led her, still totally naked, except for the boots, to the bar's entrance. He led her down the hall with the other three officers following behind, then opened another door.

She followed Derek into the room and across to a jail cell, which he unlocked and took her inside. He unfastened one cuff, then fastened it around one of the bars. Liam clamped his handcuffs around her other wrist and attached it to another bar. Jonas handcuffed one of her ankles to a bar, too, and Sloan grasped her other ankle and drew her legs apart, then cuffed her other ankle to a bar. The men then left the cell and Derek locked the door. She watched them each pour a cup of coffee and sit down in the room outside the cell, two of them on a couch and the other two in armchairs.

She stood naked, her arms and legs spread and chained. She curled her fingers around the cold metal bars and leaned forward, her breasts pushing between the bars, the nipples peaking outward.

"How about we take turns watching the prisoner?" Jonas said. "I'll go first."

"Sounds good," Derek said, and stood up.

The others followed suit and filed from the room. As soon as the door closed, Jonas stood up and approached the cell. His hot gaze wandered up and down her body, and she could see the bulge in his dark blue pants.

"You look a little uncomfortable like that." He dragged his finger down the metal bar near her left breast, then over her nipple.

She arched forward at his light touch.

"It is a little awkward," she agreed.

He stroked over her other breast, then smiled and leaned down to lick her nipple. She drew in a deep breath at the feel of his tongue lapping over her sensitive nub. Then he wrapped his lips around it and drew on it. Thrilling sensations quivered through her.

"I could probably be persuaded to remove the cuffs." He shifted to her other nipple and sucked lightly.

"Oh . . . yes?"

"That's right." He stood up again, but his hand stroked over one thigh, then around the bars, and his fingers slid between her legs.

He stroked, then glided his finger inside her. It swirled around and she ground her pelvis into the bars, opening to him as best she could.

"What . . . oh." The feel of his finger inside her sent heat melting through her. "What persuasion?"

He smiled and stepped back, then unzipped his fly and drew out his erection. It was long and hard, and it curved to the right. She wanted to wrap her hands around it and stroke it, but her wrists were attached to the bars and too far from it. She sank downward until she crouched in front of him as he pressed his cock through the bars. Hungrily, she wrapped her lips around him and swallowed his cockhead.

"What's going on?"

She glanced up to see Derek standing inside the open doorway. He stepped inside and closed the door behind him.

"The prisoner is trying to persuade me to release her from the handcuffs," Jonas answered.

Derek stepped close to the bars and unzipped his pants. "Really? Well, she'll have a little more persuading to do."

He pressed his swollen cock through the bars, too. She gazed at his erection, the veins bulging along the sides, and withdrew from Jonas' cock and wrapped her lips around Derek's. She licked his cockhead, then glided down on him. She bobbed up and down a few times, then returned to Jonas' cock and took him in her mouth, gliding down, taking all of him in her mouth.

Derek stroked her breast, then tweaked the nipple.

"Oh, yeah, honey. That's great." Jonas arched his hips forward, pushing his cock deeper into her mouth.

She sucked and squeezed him, then drew back and captured Derek again. His big cockhead filled her mouth and she glided down, taking him deep. She heard the cell door open, then clang closed again. With Derek's big shaft still in her mouth, she glanced sideways to see Jonas inside the cell, walking toward her. He stepped behind her and stroked her shoulders, then drew her upward.

Derek's cock slipped from her mouth as she stood up. Derek leaned forward and took one of her nipples in his mouth and sucked. Jonas stroked her shoulder with one hand and Derek switched to her other nipple and teased it with his lips and tongue, then began to suck. She arched against him and moaned at the pulsing sensation as he sucked harder. His other hand glided down her stomach, then his fingers slipped between her legs. He flicked over her clit and she gasped.

Jonas pressed his body against hers, his shaft pushing against her naked behind, then guided his cockhead between her cheeks. The slick head pushed against her opening. As he eased inside, she realized he'd applied lubricant. Derek stroked her clit again, sending heat thrumming through her, and Jonas glided all the way in, filling her.

Derek stood up and pressed his tip to her wet opening. He moved forward and his cock glided inside her slowly but steadily, until he, too, filled her. He stopped, his body pressed against hers, Jonas against her back. They stood like that for a moment, her face pressed against the cold hard bars, two hot hard bodies pressing against her, two hot hard cocks inside her. Her hands still held the bars, thank heavens, or she'd have melted to the floor.

Derek drew back, slowly, his corona dragging against her inner passage, stroking the sensitive flesh. Then he glided forward. Jonas also drew back and slid forward. The two of them moved in and out of her, filling her, then drawing away, then filling her again. Their rhythm increased and she gasped for air as they filled her again and again. Hot hard bodies and cold metal bars bombarded her senses as they pounded her against the bars, and each other.

She sucked in air as pleasure bounded through her, then accelerated in time with their steadily increasing thrusts. She gasped and exploded in orgasm, stiffening and clinging to the bars as they continued to thrust. Jonas groaned in release, then Derek. They both collapsed against her.

After a moment, Jonas stroked her shoulder and kissed her neck before drawing away. He grasped her right wrist, and a second later she heard the lock unlatch and he opened the cuff. Derek found her lips and kissed her through the bars, then winked at her. Then he unfastened her other wrist and tucked his handcuffs into his leather pouch while Jonas freed her ankles.

"There you go, miss." Jonas stood up, three pairs of handcuffs dangling from his hand. He opened the cell door and stepped out, then locked it behind him.

Derek crossed to a small fridge on one wall and pulled out a bottle of water, then handed it to her between the bars. She opened the bottle and took a deep swallow, then twisted the cap back on as she watched Derek and Jonas, their uniforms straightened up again, sit on the couch.

Would Liam and Sloan show up soon for their turn? Even though she'd just had a brilliant orgasm, she already anticipated their attention.

"If you're cold, there's a blanket on the cot." Derek grinned as he stared at her nipples, already stiffening in arousal.

She turned and walked to the cot, but simply sat down and drank her water. Derek picked up a deck of cards from the rectangular table in front of the couch and dealt out a hand, then he and Jonas played for a while. Janine finished her water and unzipped her boots and tugged them off, then sank back against the wall. What were Sloan and Liam doing right now?

Sloan stared at the monitor with the image of Janine totally naked in the jail cell, his cock throbbing. It had been such a wild turn-on watching the two men fuck her silly. He wanted to race down the hall to the cell right now and satisfy the feral lust boiling through him.

God damn, but there were definite advantages to being in a relationship like this. The deeply tender moments he spent with her alone were something he cherished, but sharing these intensely erotic adventures added an electrifying element to the relationship.

Liam sat on the chair beside him, also watching while he sipped his beer.

"She's one sensational woman." Liam set down his beer bottle. "There aren't a lot who are as open as she is to fun and games like this."

"That's true," Sloan said in an even voice.

Sloan realized his attitude was changing. He had watched the whole scene with Derek and Jonas, and he'd been able to handle it just fine. In fact, from the time she'd taken their hard cocks in her mouth through the bars, he'd been sporting a huge hard-on as a result, aching to go in there and thrust into her himself.

Man, could he really accept a relationship with Janine and other men at the same time? For the first time, he started to believe it was possible.

Janine sat on the cot, her pert, round breasts so inviting, her pussy, with the golden star-shaped patch of curls, so incredibly tempting. Her fingers on her thigh seemed restless, as though she wanted to stroke between her legs. Of course, that was probably hopeful thinking on his part. On the other hand, her rosy nipples were hard and distended. It could be that she was cold, but it was more exciting to assume it was because she was turned-on and waiting for the next bit of action.

"Why don't you go in there and relieve Derek and Jonas? Our girl looks like she's getting a bit bored," Sloan said.

Liam grinned. "You want me to go warm her up with a good cop routine, then you can come in with a badass attitude?"

"Sounds good to me."

Sloan watched Liam leave the room, a little unnerved. Why was it that the glint in Liam's eyes when he'd talked about warming up Janine had set Sloan's teeth on edge?

Janine glanced at the door as it opened, then Liam stepped into the room, tall and devastatingly handsome in his uniform.

Of course, they were all tall and sexy, but Liam set her heart thumping wildly.

"My turn to watch the prisoner," Liam said.

Derek tossed down his cards and grinned. "That's okay with me. Jonas was winning anyway."

Jonas and Derek stood up, then headed to the door. Derek flashed Janine a grin just before he closed the door behind him.

Liam walked toward the cell, his gaze locked on her face. "So you got yourself arrested after all."

An allusion to the previous time they'd played cop and prisoner. She smiled. "Officer O'Neill."

"I tried to talk the captain into letting you go, but he ran a check on your license and found you have a slew of unpaid traffic tickets. In addition to the nudity charge, he thinks you should stay put."

"So"—she stroked her hand along her upper arm, then under her breast—"there's nothing I can do to convince you to let me out of here?"

"Well, I didn't say that. Maybe if you're very cooperative, I could convince him to reconsider."

Hormones flooded through her and she widened her legs and cupped her breast. "I can be very cooperative."

He smiled. "Yes, I remember."

Liam's gaze locked on her breasts as she squeezed them, then pressed them together. Her soft flesh swelled forward, and her nipples peeked out from between her fingers. She drew her hands down her torso, stroking her silky flesh, then stroked up over her breasts, continuing over her shoulders and back down her arms.

She turned and lay down on the cot. His cock swelled painfully in his pants as she stroked up and down her body, teasing her nipples, then stroking down her stomach, then back up. She pinched her hard nipples. He could imagine the tight little buds between his own fingertips and almost groaned. As she cupped a breast with one hand, the other traveled down to her golden pubic hairs, trimmed into that cute little star shape, and petted for a moment before drifting lower. He sucked in a breath as her fingers glided over the folds between her legs.

He watched as the tip of her finger dipped into her slit, then pushed inside. As she pressed her finger in and out, he could imagine her soft, velvety opening around his fingers.

"What does it feel like?" His gaze, locked on her moving finger, left no doubt what he was asking.

"Hot and wet."

Unable to stand it any longer, he grabbed the key Derek had left on the coffee table and opened the door, then walked toward her. She watched him approach with half-lidded eyes. She slid a second finger inside as he sat on the cot beside her.

"Are you going to touch me, Officer O'Neill?" she asked in a throaty voice.

"Yes." He cupped her breast. The soft flesh filled his hand and the tight bud pressed into his palm.

God, she had a delightful body. He watched her two fingers push in and out of her slit as he dragged his hand from her warm breast and trailed it down her stomach. Then he stroked the star with his fingertips. He longed to be inside that sweet pussy of hers.

He leaned down and captured a distended nipple in his mouth. His tongue found the tight, pebbly aureola and stroked it. She moaned softly. He licked, then sucked, drawing the hard nub deep into his mouth. Her fingers forked through his hair as he continued to pull on her nipple, and soft sounds emanated from her throat.

He ached to be inside her . . . but first he wanted to taste her. He stood up and moved to the end of the cot. He knelt down and wrapped his hands around her legs, then pulled her downward until her calves draped over the end, her feet resting on the floor. He pressed her thighs wide and leaned toward her. He grasped her hand and drew it from her depths, then wrapped his lips around her slick fingers and sucked. Releasing them, he leaned forward and licked the length of her slick folds. He pressed his tongue to her opening and pushed it inside, tasting her sweet femininity.

He probed along her slit with his fingers until he found her clit, then pulled the fleshy folds apart so he could see it. He dragged his tongue toward it, then lapped over the tiny button. She sucked in air, her fingers moving through his hair as she arched against him.

He drew away and smiled up at her. "You like that?"

"Yes, Officer O'Neill."

"You want me to keep doing it?"

"Yes, please, Officer O'Neill."

He chuckled, then licked her again. At her soft moan, his gut tightened. He loved giving her pleasure.

He stroked her clitoris with his tongue, savoring her murmurs of delight. His fingers slipped inside her and he stroked as he continued to tease her sensitive nub with his mouth. She arched against him, her fingers twisting in his hair. He stroked faster and sucked on her clit. She moaned, then writhed beneath him as he twirled his fingers inside and flicked his tongue rapidly over her clit.

Finally, she wailed her release.

Once she collapsed on the cot, he stood up and moved to the side of it. She smiled and sat up, then ran her fingers over the straining bulge in his pants. She tugged his zipper down and reached inside.

Tingles raced through him as her warm hand closed around his aching cock. She drew it out, then gazed at it lovingly as she stroked it. His heart thundered in his chest as she leaned forward and kissed his tip. She licked, then wrapped her soft lips around him and glided downward until her lips tucked under his corona, his whole cockhead in her mouth. Her tongue swirled over him. Intense need shuddered through him. He wanted to thrust forward, filling her with his cock, but he held still.

Her fingers found his balls and she stroked them. She glided down his cock, taking more and more of his shaft in her mouth, until she'd taken his whole length. God, she was good at this.

He stroked her hair as she bobbed up and down on his cock. Her hot mouth around him, her tongue teasing his shaft, her hands cradling his balls— all combined to send his senses soaring. Heat pumped through him. He sucked in a breath as she took him impossibly deep, then moved faster on him, squeezing him in her mouth. Pleasure speared through his entire body and he erupted into her mouth.

He stroked the long, blond hair back from her face and she released his spent cock.

Janine gazed up at him with impish blue eyes and the sheer beauty of her unabashedly sexy smile took his breath away. He pulled her to her feet and gazed into her eyes.

"You are incredible."

Her eyes widened a little and her smile turned almost timid.

"Thank you, Officer O'Neill."

He chuckled, then dragged her against his body and captured her lips, spearing his tongue into her sweet mouth. He kissed her deeply, and thoroughly.

"You know, you are a very cooperative prisoner." He grabbed her wrists and backed her up against the cell wall, pinning her hands above her head. "You know, sometimes an *un*cooperative prisoner is more fun."

A flicker of a smile crossed her lips, and she gazed up at him with wide eyes filled with mock concern. "What are you doing, Officer? I did what you wanted. Aren't you going to let me go yet?"

"Why should I let you go when I can have all the fun with you I want right here?"

She arched her naked body against him. "No, you mustn't take advantage of me."

Despite his release only moments before, the feel of her naked body arching against him as she struggled sent his cock swelling. He drew her arms farther apart and leaned down to cover her nipple with his mouth. He dragged his tongue over her pebbly aureola and licked, then sucked mercilessly. She whimpered. Her hard bud swelled in his mouth. He licked and sucked again.

She writhed against him and his cock pressed against her stomach as it hardened even more.

"Officer, please. Don't fuck me."

He pressed his body tight against her. "Why not?"

Janine stared into Liam's gleaming eyes as he asked her the question. She couldn't think of a single reason, especially since she so sincerely *wanted* him to fuck her. Right now.

His rock-hard cock against her stomach made her insides ache with intense yearning.

"You just can't," she finally managed to say.

He leaned in close to her face. "Well, now, that sounds like a challenge."

He pulled her wrists down and drew her across the cell, then twisted her around. Suddenly she felt cold metal against her wrists, and a second later she found herself pressed against the bars with her wrists cuffed through them. Liam's body pressed against her thighs, and she felt his cockhead glide along her slick opening. The hard flesh burned against her and painful pleasure spiked through her as she longed for him to drive into her.

"You are a very *bad* girl, and I'm going to treat you like one," he said, then thrust forward.

She gasped as his hard flesh invaded her body, thrilling her as it drove deep.

"Oh, God." She wrapped her fingers around the bars as she stared unseeingly at the wall beyond, barely aware of anything but the huge shaft of flesh filling her.

He pulled back and drove forward again, crushing her naked body against the cold bars.

"Oh, Officer, you mustn't—"

He pulled back and filled her again. She moaned.

He drove into her again and again, in accelerated thrusts. Pleasure rocketed through her, and she wailed as intense pleasure shot through her.

Finally she collapsed against the bars, his body tight against her, his cock still fully immersed in her . . . and still as hard as a rock.

He kissed her cheek, then drew back, his cockhead stroking along her inner channel almost setting her off again.

He unfastened her wrists and turned her around, then captured her lips in a sweet, passionate kiss.

Sloan stared at the camera, his gazed locked on the expression on Liam's face. He looked like a man . . . oh, God . . . totally smitten by a woman.

As Liam continued to kiss Janine, he backed her toward the cot. He lay her down gently and prowled over her.

Suddenly, the scene seemed way too intimate for Sloan's liking. Maybe he couldn't handle this after all.

Eighteen

Sloan's heart ached, knowing the only alternative was giving up on Janine, and he couldn't do that. The only chance he had of possibly winning her for good—of making this work—was to prove to her that he accepted her for who she was. Even if she made love to his best friend.

Sloan turned and strode to the door, then hurried down the hall to the room with the cell. Janine and Liam lay on the cot, their naked bodies still entwined, catching their breath.

"Officer O'Neill," Sloan snapped.

Liam gazed around. "Yes, Captain?"

"You're out of uniform."

"Sorry, Captain." Liam leaned down and kissed Janine, then lifted himself from her body. He took her hand and helped her to sit up, then picked up his uniform from the floor and began putting it on.

Once he'd finished putting on his clothes, he sat on the cot and pulled on his shoes, then glanced toward Sloan.

"I told the prisoner I would try to persuade you to be

lenient and let her go," Liam said. "I think if you spend a little time with her, she might convince you to set her free."

"I think you might be right," Sloan said.

He strode to the cot and grasped her hands, then drew her to her feet and into his arms. He captured her lips and stormed her mouth in a deep, demanding kiss. His tongue drove into her and found her tongue, then swirled over it. Her wide eyes fell closed and her arms surrounded him. He stroked her back as their mouths moved together passionately.

Her fingers tangled in his shirt buttons as she tried to unfasten them. He separated from her briefly to tug the shirt over his shoulders and toss it aside, then pulled her to him again. He sucked in a breath as her soft breasts pressed against his naked skin. His cock swelled painfully.

With their lips still locked together, she released his zipper. He shoved his pants down, boxers and all, and kicked them away, then backed her to the wall. He wrapped his hand around his erection, which was pushing against her belly, and guided it to her opening.

Janine gasped as Sloan's huge cock thrust into her, pinning her to the wall. His intense blue eyes stared into hers and she felt his love washing over her. She pressed her lips to his again, lost in a sea of emotion. Hot, tumultuous feelings of lust, confusion, even a little fear—but mostly of love—for this warm, loving, yet frustrating man.

But, by God, she needed him.

He drew back, his big cock stroking her inner passage, driving her so wild she trembled. Then he thrust deep again.

"Oh, God, Sloan. That feels so good." She kissed him again, desperate for him to possess her completely.

He pulled back and drove deep again, filling her body with his awesome cock—and filling her soul with love.

He plunged into her again and again. Pleasure swelled, bursting through every cell, flooding each nerve ending. She gasped as rapture swept through her, carrying her to a place of infinite joy. She clung to him, wailing, barely hearing the sound of her own voice as it careened higher and higher, leaving her voice hoarse.

She flew over the edge to a place of unspeakable ecstasy.

Sloan groaned . . . and followed her to that state of pure bliss.

"Officer O'Neill. Get the hell out of here." Sloan still held Janine tight to his body, his cock still embedded inside her.

"Is there something wrong, Sloan?" Liam asked.

"No, just . . . go get the others and go back to the bar. Ensure we've got privacy here."

"Okay. Sure."

Sloan didn't want the others watching him and Janine. The door closed behind Liam.

"Sloan—"

"Wait."

He held her pressed between his body and the wall. It should take only another couple of minutes.

A knock sounded at the door.

"What is it?" Sloan called.

"Cameras and audio are off," Liam called from the other side of the door.

"Thanks," Sloan said. "Whoever wasn't in the room with you was watching a video feed."

She nodded. "I figured."

He drew back from her, immediately missing her soft body pressed against his. He strode to the cot and tugged the blanket from the top, then walked back to her and draped it over her shoulders. She grasped it and pulled it closed around her, covering her lovely body.

"Is something wrong, Sloan?"

"No. Well . . ." He raked a hand through his hair. "I'm sorry, but I need to know. The way Liam was looking at you . . . Is there something going on between you two?"

She pursed her lips. "Sloan, there's something going on between me and all the guys here. Including you."

His lips compressed to a flat line. "Let me be clearer, then. Have you been seeing him outside the group?"

Irritation flared through Janine. "There's no reason I should feel guilty about that." Even though she did. "You knew the deal before we started this."

His jaw tensed and his eyes glittered like granite. "Are you in love with Liam?"

She opened her mouth to deny it, then closed it again. The fact that he'd ask her that, and with so much emotion in his eyes, was the proof that she'd been looking for all along. Proof that he couldn't handle any of this.

Sloan frowned, clearly taking her hesitation as an answer. Anger flared in his eyes and he turned his back on her. In total silence, he gathered his clothes and pulled them on, then left the cell, leaving the door open behind him. He strode out of the room. Janine stared at the door, her irritation ebbing away. Damn. She'd made a huge mistake starting this with Sloan. All along, she'd been afraid he'd get hurt, but it had seemed the only way to convince him there would never be anything more between them than friendship.

Now she wondered if even that would remain.

Nineteen

In a daze, Janine pulled the blanket around her, then walked across the room and out the door into the hallway. She went upstairs to the bedroom where she'd left her suitcase and pulled on a pair of jeans and a T-shirt, then headed back downstairs to the bar. As soon as she opened the door, three pairs of eyes turned to her.

"Sloan left," she said.

Liam stood up and approached her. "What's going on with him?"

"He was . . . upset about something." She gazed at Liam, then Derek and Jonas. "I'm sorry, but I'd like to go home."

"Of course. No problem," Derek said. "You go ahead and pack up your stuff. We'll handle everything else."

An hour later, they piled the last of the suitcases into the two cars. Sloan must have hitched a ride to the nearby town, since they'd driven up in Liam's and Derek's cars and both were still there.

"You want to ride with me?" Liam asked.

Janine nodded. Derek and Jonas each gave her a warm hug and a kiss.

She gazed at Jonas. "Sorry I'm cutting our weekend short."

He stroked her cheek and smiled. "Don't worry. There's always next time."

She nodded, and Liam opened the passenger door of his car for her and she climbed in. She waved at the other two men as Liam pulled away.

Not really wanting to talk, she reclined her seat and closed her eyes. It was only an hour and a half back to town, and Liam respected her obvious desire to ride home in silence. As they reached the city limits, however, she tilted her seat up again and glanced around. She really didn't want to go home to her empty apartment, where she'd think about Sloan all night long.

She glanced at Liam's profile. Liam was a really special guy, but she wasn't in love with him. It was better that way. She didn't understand love at all. The only thing it ever seemed to do was mess things up and break her heart.

Liam turned onto her street, then into her apartment building entrance. He stopped in front of the main door.

"I'll help you carry your stuff up," he said.

"Actually . . ." She turned and gazed at him. "Do you want to spend the night?"

He smiled warmly. "I'd love to spend the night."

Sloan closed his front door and kicked off his shoes, then tossed his keys in the bowl by the front door. Usually, he'd toss his cell phone there, too, but he'd left it behind when he'd rushed out. Hopefully, Liam would notice it and bring it back.

He slung his jacket across the back of his big leather arm-chair on his way to the bedroom. Exhaustion ached through him, more from emotional turmoil than from physical exer-tion, though it had been about a five-mile walk from the dun-geon cottage to the nearest town, where he'd caught the bus back.

Damn, he'd really blown it. He tugged off his clothes and uncharacteristically tossed them in a heap on the floor, then climbed into bed. Everything had been going so well. He'd coped well with—in fact, enjoyed—most of the evening. Watching Janine with Derrick and Jonas had set his hormones aflame. His cock twitched at the memory. But when he'd seen the look in Liam's eyes as he'd made love to Janine . . .

God damn, but how was he to cope with another man emotionally connecting with his woman?

But Janine wasn't his woman. In fact, if she were here, she'd tell him in no uncertain terms that she'd never agree to be anyone's woman.

He turned off the bedside lamp. Moonlight glowed in the window, casting his room in a cool, blue light. The room felt desolate and lonely. He stared at the ceiling.

Could it be that he had overreacted tonight?

Maybe Janine wasn't really in love with Liam. She hadn't actually answered Sloan when he'd asked her. He'd simply jumped to that conclusion because of her hesitation. Because of his insecurity, he'd read that as a guilty admission, but maybe she'd simply been taken aback by his suggestion.

Hope rose in him as he realized that maybe the sugges-tion had simply taken her by surprise.

Damn it. Jealousy had gotten the better of him and now she'd be totally convinced he could never handle her lifestyle.

And for good reason.

He'd begun to wonder if he could ever get to the point where he could handle it. It was one thing for her to have a little fun, and he found it amazingly hot to watch her with the other men, but he had never actually thought about the fact that she might form a real connection with one of them. If that weren't a possibility, maybe he could get to the point where he and Janine could be a couple, with other men joining them in the bedroom. They could even get married. It was somewhat unconventional, but he could learn to live with that. Could he, however, learn to accept that she might form an emotional attachment to one of those men?

Liam drove past the door to visitors' parking. Moments later, he and Janine got off the elevator and walked down the hall to her apartment door.

Once inside, Liam carried her bags into the bedroom, then returned to the living room.

"Want something to drink?" she asked.

"Yeah. Just water will be fine."

Janine walked into the kitchen, then returned with two tall glasses of ice water. Liam had settled on the couch and she sat beside him, setting his water on the table.

"So what happened with you and Sloan?" he asked as he picked up his glass.

She sipped and set hers down. How could she explain that Sloan was mad because he believed she was in love with Liam?

"Well, umm . . ." She gazed at Liam. "It seems that . . ." She shrugged and stared at her glass. "Well, Sloan seems to have got it into his head that there's something special between us. He even asked me if I'm in love with you." She picked up her glass again and stared at the ice cubes floating in the water. "Crazy, right?"

Liam watched Janine as she stared at her glass, purposely not gazing in his direction.

He took the glass from her hand and set it on the table. "Actually, it's not so crazy. Sloan has great instincts."

Janine turned her head and met Liam's gaze. In her bright blue eyes shone a question.

He tucked his fingers under her chin and tipped up her head, then met her lips with his own. The feel of her soft mouth under his sent his heart thundering. He wrapped his arms around her and drew her close as his tongue dipped into her mouth, tasting her sweetness. Her tongue stroked his and the two danced in unison, setting a fire ablaze within him.

He stroked her hair from her face and drew back, locking gazes with her.

"I think there *is* something special between us."

In fact, he wondered if he *was* falling for her. He captured her mouth again, reveling in the feel of her soft lips under his.

"Maybe Sloan can't handle your lifestyle, but I can. Sloan is a good friend of mine—don't get me wrong. But if you two aren't right for each other, and we are, then why should the two of us deny ourselves happiness?"

"Liam, I—"

He placed a finger over her lips. "Shh. Let's not think

about Sloan tonight. You and I are here alone. Let's just enjoy being with each other, and think about the rest of the world tomorrow."

Janine gazed into Liam's deep olive green eyes. Surely he didn't think he was falling in love with her. Should she say something? Straighten things out right now?

But, then, maybe she was reading too much into his words. He'd simply said there was something special between them.

As he leaned in to kiss her, she realized that she wanted to do exactly as he'd suggested, to put aside her worries and just be with him. Cared for and cherished. With no expectations.

As his lips met hers, she wrapped her arms around him. His tongue stroked inside her and she melted against him. She drew his tongue deeper into her mouth and sucked lightly. He groaned, then drove his tongue deeper still.

She leaned back and tugged at the hem of her camisole, then pulled it over her head. Liam's gaze on her black-lace-clad breasts sent heat shimmering through her. She reached behind her and unhooked the bra, then pulled down the straps and glided her arms free, leaving the garment covering her breasts.

He smiled and kissed her neck, then downward, over the swell of her breasts. He tucked a finger under the loose cup, then drew it down slowly, until her nipple peeked over the fabric. He ran his fingertip over the sensitive bud and it swelled. He drew the other cup downward until both nipples peered at him. He took one between his fingertips and rolled it around, then leaned down and licked it. He sucked, and the intense sensation lanced through her. She wrapped her hands around his head, her fingers forking through his short, sandy hair, pulling him tight to her. He sucked again, harder this time. She gasped. Her vagina contracted, aching with need.

He drew the bra away and stroked her breasts lovingly. Then he cupped one and kissed and licked the other until she squirmed beneath him. He switched to the other breast, enveloping the abandoned one with his warm hand. Then he glided down her stomach and kissed her navel, and with a half smile on his lips, he unbuttoned her jeans and glided the zipper down slowly.

She lifted her hips as he tugged her jeans down and pulled them off her legs, leaving her in only her skimpy black lace panties. He dropped her jeans to the floor, then smiled as his gaze lingered on the black lace covering her. He lowered his head and fluttered his lips against the skin above the lace in delicate kisses, then grasped the lace between his teeth and tugged downward, slowly revealing the trimmed curls. He nibbled sideways along the top of the panties, then tugged them down one hip, leaving her panties skewed across her body, low on one side and clinging to her hip on the other. He released them, kissed back to her navel, then ran his tongue through the star-shaped curls.

She tucked her fingers under the high side of her panties and rolled them downward, wanting him to move lower. He chuckled and grasped the front of her panties with his fingers, then slowly drew them down, revealing more of her. Finally, he pulled the crotch all the way down, exposing all of her, then he tugged them down her legs and tossed them aside.

He stroked through the star, then downward, stopping above her slit.

"You have a cute little pussy."

She opened her legs, propping her feet on the edge of the couch, opening wide for him.

"Show me how much you like it."

He laughed and knelt on the floor, positioning himself between her thighs.

"My pleasure." He tucked his thumbs against her fleshy folds and drew them apart. Then he leaned forward and licked the length of her slit.

"Oh, yes." Her head dropped against the back of the couch as pleasure quivered through her.

He licked, and licked again. Then his tongue found her clit and he pressed the tip of his tongue against it lightly. At the same time, his fingertip stroked her slit. As her insides melted, her slit filled with moisture. His finger glided to her opening and slid inside. Then another finger. He stroked her inside passage as his tongue pressed harder on her clit, then rolled it around and around. She sucked in a breath at the incredible sensation.

"Oh, Liam. Yes."

He stroked inside her as he sucked on her clit. Joy swelled inside her and she trembled with need. His fingers found that magic spot inside that sent her gasping in pleasure. Her body ached with rising need. She was close.

He slid his mouth downward, then pressed his tongue inside her, too, thrusting in and out. Then he returned to her clit and sucked in a pulsing rhythm. She gasped, then clung to him as she rode the wave of ecstasy, moaning her release. He stroked and sucked, stroked and sucked, until she gasped one last time, then slumped on the couch.

"Oh, my God. That was incredible." She sighed happily.

He smiled. "Honey, you ain't seen nothing yet."

He tucked his arms under her legs and shoulders and lifted her. She wrapped her arms around his neck as he carried her into the bedroom.

He set her on the bed gently, then leaned in and kissed her—a sweet, cherishing kiss. His mouth lingered. Then he stood up and unfastened the buttons of his shirt. She licked her lips as she watched the shirt part, revealing solid muscle beneath. As he drew the shirt open and glided it down his arms, his ridged abs rippled. She covered her breasts with her hands and stroked, then tweaked the nipples. His green eyes burned into her as he released the zipper on his jeans and dropped them to the floor. His big cock swelled out the top of his boxers. He tucked his thumbs in the waistband and pushed them to the floor, then stepped out of them, revealing his big, naked erection. She wriggled on the bed, wanting that huge shaft inside her. She stroked between her legs, totally soaked from the slickness of her intense arousal.

"Don't get too far ahead of me, sweetheart."

He sat on the bed and ran his hand over her fingers as she stroked her hot flesh. He guided her hand toward him and drew her fingers into his mouth.

"Mmm. Delicious."

She sat up and wrapped her fingers around his huge erection, longing to taste it.

"Here, let me catch you up." She leaned forward and licked the tip of him, then wrapped her lips around the mushroom-shaped head and took it in her mouth.

She lapped at him, then sucked. He groaned as she glided downward, taking him deeper. She tucked her hands under his testicles and stroked them as she bobbed up and down on his hard cock.

"Oh, yeah. That feels—" He groaned again, then grasped her head and stilled her movement. He drew his cock from her mouth.

"That feels incredible, but right now I want to do this." He leaned down and suckled on her nipple, sending swirls of pleasure spiraling through her.

Her hand stroked down his tight stomach until she brushed against his hot, hard shaft, still damp from her mouth, and she wrapped her fingers around it. "Fuck me, Liam."

He smiled but shook his head. "No. I'm not going to fuck you. I'm going to make slow, passionate love to you until I set your whole world on end."

He grasped her wrists and drew them above her head, then held them there with one hand. With the other, he stroked her wet slit, then teased her clit with his fingers. She sucked in a breath at the intense sensations. He pressed his cockhead to her opening and glided it up and down, stroking her. She arched her pelvis forward and he chuckled, then leaned down and kissed her.

"Anxious, are we?" He kissed her again, then pressed his cock forward.

Slowly, it pushed into her. First, his cockhead pressed inside, and he stayed poised like that, smiling at her. Her insides ached for him. She wiggled a little, trying to get him deeper. He grinned, then began to move forward slowly, filling her a little at a time.

She sucked in air, loving the feel of his big, hard cock gliding into her, deeper and deeper. Then he thrust the last little bit and she gasped. Her internal muscles clenched around him, like a tight, erotic hug. Instead of pulling back and thrusting, he stayed deep inside her. She gazed up at him and almost gasped at the warm, loving look in his olive green eyes. That look touched something deep inside her.

His lips brushed lightly against her, then across her cheek and her forehead. Then he captured her mouth and his lips moved on hers with a depth of passion that took her breath away. He drew back and glided into her again, his mouth still locked to hers. Then again. Drawing back and thrusting. Back and thrusting. Filling her with his big cock. His mouth moving on hers, his tongue engaging hers in an erotic dance.

Sensations swirled around her and through her. Passion, lust, pleasure, tenderness.

He thrust again. She pulled her mouth free and gasped. He nuzzled her neck and she arched her body, lurching against his hand still grasping her wrists. She felt mastered but cared for and cherished at the same time. He drove deep and swirled inside her, then drew back and thrust again.

Pleasure rippled through her, then swelled. She gasped again at his next thrust and moaned.

"Oh, God, Janine." He kissed her again. "I love you."

His cock drove into her again.

"I . . . Oh . . ." God, what could she say?

She gasped as he drove deep again. Her thoughts melted away.

Another thrust and joy blasted through her. "Oh, God, that's so good."

"Good, huh?" he said with an unreadable grin. He thrust faster and deeper. Her joy turned to ecstasy as she clung to him and catapulted to heaven.

He groaned and thrust forward one more time, pinning her to the bed as he shuddered, releasing inside her. Finally, he collapsed on her and they clung to each other, gasping.

After a moment, he rolled to his side and drew her tight to his body. He kissed her. Tenderly. Sweetly. As the fire subsided and Janine caught her breath, his words echoed through her mind.

I love you.

Oh, man. What was she going to do now?

Twenty

Janine set down her cell phone, having just finished typing in a text message to Sloan. One of several this morning. She wrapped her hands around her warm coffee cup and took a sip as she gazed out the big living room window, not seeing the view beyond.

She was worried about Sloan. He'd disappeared into the night, out in the middle of nowhere. Something could have happened to him. He could have been hit by a car, or murdered, or . . .

Her heart thundered in her chest and she sucked in a deep breath. She knew she was being silly. Sloan could take care of himself. He was a cop, for heaven's sake.

But then, Ben had been, too.

Her chest compressed. God, if anything happened to Sloan . . . She couldn't lose him, too.

She picked up her cell and checked for messages again, to ensure she hadn't missed his response. Nothing.

Maybe he was just mad at her. Or, more likely, he was hurt and needed some space.

Damn it, had she screwed everything up?

"Hey, you look like you're deep in thought." Liam sat down beside her and laid his arm against the back of the couch so his hand curled around her shoulder.

"I have a lot to think about." She stared at the black coffee in her cup.

"About us . . . or about Sloan?"

She hesitated. *Both.* But she didn't want to tell him that.

He drew her close and captured her lips. "You and I should talk about last night. How we feel about each other. And where this is going."

She smiled. "Gee, a guy who's willing to talk about the relationship. That's novel."

Except that Sloan wanted to talk about the relationship, too. Unfortunately, she had no answers for Sloan. At least not ones he wanted to hear.

Not that she knew what answers she'd have for Liam. Why did relationships have to be so complicated? Up until now, she'd been able to keep them simple. Casual.

But now that Sloan and Liam had started to pursue her, her whole sense of what a relationship should be—at least for her—was spinning out of control, like a merry-go-round on steroids, leaving her dizzy and disoriented.

"Okay, let's talk," she said. "But first I need to ask you something."

"Okay."

"What do you think about the fact that I have sex with Derek and Jonas and . . . ?" She hesitated.

"And Sloan?"

She nodded.

"Well, it's pretty hot."

"You don't think there's anything wrong with it?"

"Of course not. All of you obviously have a strong mutual respect and a lot of affection for each other. And you don't just grab any guy off the street and jump in the sack with him, I assume."

"When I first had sex with you, I didn't even know who you were." She stared at her cup, swirling the liquid around inside it.

"Yeah, but that was a stranger fantasy and you trusted Sloan's judgment. And Sloan is exceptionally trustworthy."

"A lot of people would think that I'm . . . a little reckless."

"Look, sweetheart. When it all comes down to it, it's just sex. There's nothing wrong with a little recreational sex. And living out your fantasies." He grinned. "That's incredibly exciting." He tipped up her chin and gazed into her uncertain blue eyes. "And I think when you find you want a deeper relationship, you'll make some man . . . or men . . . very happy."

Her eyes widened.

"So you'd be . . . open to a long-term relationship with me . . . and other men?"

"I want to be with you. If you want to be with me, too, long-term . . . then we'll figure it out."

"I . . . um . . . last night, when you said . . ."

"When I said 'I love you' and you said 'that's so good'? Or were you just commenting on my technique?"

"I . . ." She took his hands in hers. "I have to be honest with you. I think the world of you, but . . ." Oh, damn, how could she say this?

The gleam in his eyes faded and he slumped a little. "Oh, boy. Here it comes."

She squeezed his hands. "Liam, you just got out of a

long-term relationship. Isn't it possible you're just a little eager to find someone? That you really want to be in a relationship so you've convinced yourself you're in love with me?"

He stroked her hair from her face, tucking it behind one ear with a gentleness that touched her heart. "Janine, you're a very special woman. I don't have to convince myself to love you."

She tipped her head and smiled. "That's very sweet, and I told you I feel something special for you, too, but it's not love. Isn't it possible that what you feel for me isn't love, either?"

His lips compressed and he shook his head slowly. "I don't know. I just know that I don't want to let you go. I want to keep seeing you." He drew her closer, his green eyes staring deeply into hers, and cupped her cheek. "To keep touching you, and holding you."

She smiled. "And making love to me."

"And definitely making love to you."

She leaned forward and kissed him. A sweet, tender kiss. "And I want that, too. We have a very special connection." She kissed him again. "But not love. Okay?"

He nodded. "Maybe I was a little overzealous. I've just never met anyone like you before." He leaned back. "So let me ask you something."

"What's that?"

"Are you in love with Sloan?"

Her heart thundered in her chest at his words. She pursed her lips. "That's . . . a little complicated."

"Okay. Then let me ask this: How long has Sloan been in love with you? Because he must be, or he wouldn't have stormed off because he thinks I'm in love with you." Liam watched her expression turn guilty. "Or was it that he decided you're in love with me?"

That would have been Sloan's real worry.

"Sloan has been in love with me for a long time. He just . . . decided not to act on it until recently. When he left L.A . . ." She shrugged. "I don't think it's a coincidence he chose to come here. He wanted to start up a relationship with me. I didn't want to close him out—he and I have a lot of history—but maybe I shouldn't have allowed our relationship to become intimate. I just didn't want to turn him away and . . . I thought it was the only way to convince him that . . . you know . . . he and I would never work out."

Liam just stared at her, unable to believe his ears. He'd thought she and Sloan had known each other only for a matter of weeks—months at the outside—but now he realized she and Sloan had known each other for a long time. In fact, from the sound of things . . .

"Wait a minute. How long have you and Sloan known each other?"

She glanced at Liam.

"We grew up together, back in L.A."

"Did you . . . have a brother? Who was a cop?" he asked.

She stared at him. Her eyes shimmered slightly.

"Yeah. Ben. He . . . died several years ago."

He took her hand. "I'm sorry." He didn't like that his question had nudged her old pain, but right now he had to know. "Your brother and Sloan, they were best friends, right?"

She nodded. "How did you know?"

"I knew there was someone he'd been hung up on for years—someone from his past. I just didn't realize it was you."

She lowered her gaze. "He sure picked the wrong woman, didn't he? If it hadn't been for me, maybe he would have found someone better—someone *normal*—and he'd be a whole lot happier than he is now."

"You'd don't know that. And you do make him happy. That's why he's so hung up on you. The man is in love with you, Janine. Maybe you should let yourself love him, too."

Liam's phone blipped and he pulled it out of his pocket and stared at the display.

We need to talk. I'm at the Blue Mountain restaurant around the corner.
                                                              — *Sloan*

What the hell? Liam had Sloan's cell phone, since he'd left it behind, so Sloan must be using his Netbook. He loved that thing. But how did Sloan know Liam was here?

And what did Sloan want to talk to him about? Clearly, it was the situation with Janine, but what? Would he ask Liam to step aside and end all future involvement with Janine?

He glanced at her.

"Look, I have to go. Something's come up." He had no intention of telling her he was going to talk to Sloan. She wouldn't be happy they were going to talk about the situation without her, but Sloan and Liam couldn't really express themselves honestly if she were there.

"Okay. I guess I'll see you later," she said.

He pulled her into his arms and kissed her soundly. "You can bet on it." With that, he strode out.

Twenty-one

As soon as Liam left, Janine sank onto the sofa and simply stared at the door. *Maybe you should let yourself love him, too.*

If only it were that easy.

Oh, damn. Why the hell couldn't Sloan just move on and find someone new? Sure, they had chemistry together. Damned strong chemistry. But they didn't share the same outlook on love. They were not compatible.

Were they?

She fiddled with her ring. Could it be that she was wrong, not Sloan? Was her obsessive refusal to consider any other lifestyle a refusal to grow and evolve? Should she be moving on to a different type of relationship? Thinking about settling down and embracing one love?

She certainly didn't follow a traditional way of doing things, and if she chose to settle in and follow the norm . . . it would certainly make life easier.

And she could be with Sloan. Make him happy. And herself, too, since she really did love him.

Could she make it work with Sloan?

———

Sloan watched Liam step through the glass door into the rustic restaurant. He glanced around, then spotted Sloan and walked over. He slid onto the upholstered seat across from Sloan in the wooden booth.

"How'd you know I was at Janine's?" Liam asked.

"I saw your car in visitors' parking."

Sloan had come by to talk to Janine this morning, to see if he could square things with her. When he'd seen Liam's car, anxiety had gripped him. Liam's suitcase was still in the backseat, which meant he probably hadn't gone home. If he'd stayed the night, Sloan was sure they hadn't spent the whole time talking.

The waitress came by and poured Liam a coffee and offered him a menu.

"Just coffee," Liam said.

So, he'd already had breakfast.

Jealousy washed through Sloan, but he knew he had to conquer it. Liam spending the night didn't mean Janine was in love with him. It just meant she'd probably had sex with him. That was part of the arrangement, and Sloan had to get past his obsessive jealousy about it. Anyway, it wasn't really the sex that bothered him.

Whether Janine was in love with Liam or not, he was a reality in her life, and Sloan had to get over it.

Liam pushed the steaming coffee to one side, folded his hands on the table, and leaned forward. "Sloan, Janine and I were talking this morning and . . ." He shook his head. "I didn't realize who Janine is."

"What do you mean who she is?"

"I mean, I didn't realize she's the sister of your old friend. That she's the one you've been in love with for a long time."

What the hell? How did Liam even know about his feelings for Ben's sister?

"Come on, Sloan. I know you don't open up much, but when you told me about your friend . . . when you talked about his sister . . . it wasn't hard to figure out." His lips compressed. "I knew you were in love with her. I just didn't know she and Janine were the same person."

Sloan's eyes narrowed. "So what are you saying? That you'll step aside so I can have the girl?"

Janine paced back and forth across her living room carpet.

God, she loved Sloan. Settling in with him in a one-on-one relationship would simplify her life, and she'd really be able to give him the time and attention he deserved.

But would she be able to make it work?

She wasn't sure, but the one thing she knew was that it beat the alternative. She couldn't imagine life without Sloan.

She stared at her cell phone. She had sent several more texts to Sloan after Liam had left, but he hadn't yet responded. Was he still angry about last night? Still too hurt to talk to her?

She understood he'd probably need some time to figure things out, but she was starting to worry. She toyed with her ring. Memories of that horrible night when she'd heard about Ben . . . when they'd told her he'd been shot and killed . . .

Sure, Sloan hadn't been on duty, but he'd left on foot. He

could have been hit by a car. Robbed and shot by some thug.

Oh, God, what if something had happened to him?

She grabbed her phone again and dialed Sloan's cell. It rang, then went to voice mail. She ended the call, then tapped in a text message to him.

Call me. Please.

Her buzzer sounded and she dodged to the intercom.

"Yes?" she said, hoping to hear Sloan's voice.

"Hi, it's Liam."

Disappointment washed through her that it wasn't Sloan. She pressed the button to let him in. A few moments later, he knocked on the door and she pulled it open.

Before it could even fully register that it was Sloan standing at the door rather than Liam, he scooped her into his strong masculine arms, and his mouth covered hers in a demanding, passionate kiss. Her arms automatically wrapped around him, and her breathing accelerated. The feel of his big, hard body pressed against hers sent shivers through her. She melted against him, her tongue joining his in a dance of passion.

"Oh, my God, why didn't you answer your cell? I sent you about a million texts," she said as soon as she pulled her mouth free, but he captured it again, consuming her with the passion of his kiss.

He nuzzled her cheek. "I left my cell phone behind last night. Liam gave it back to me, but I forgot to turn it on." His hungry mouth merged with hers again.

"But Liam was—" She stopped short, not wanting to agitate a touchy situation.

"Here. I know. I saw his car in the parking lot."

So that's where Liam had gone. To see Sloan. Why hadn't he told her?

"So you had him buzz you up?" She drew back a little, gazing up at him.

"I was afraid you wouldn't want to see me."

"I told you, I've been calling and texting."

He shoved his hand in his pocket and pulled out his phone. The device glowed to life and he flicked a couple of buttons, then grinned broadly. "So you have. Did you miss me?"

"I was worried about you. I wanted to make sure you were okay."

"Is that all? You just wanted to know if I was okay?"

A lump formed in her throat. "Actually, I was afraid you might be dead."

His teasing grin faded and he wrapped his arms around her and hugged her tight. Then he drew back and gazed at her with his penetrating blue eyes. She was sure thoughts of Ben flickered through his mind, too.

"I'm sorry. I didn't mean to worry you."

She nodded, twisting her ring back and forth, afraid to speak because her voice might quiver with emotion.

"Janine, we need to talk."

She nodded, totally unsure of what she would say to him. He took her hand and led her to the couch, then they sat down.

"Janine, I know you think I won't be able to fit into your lifestyle—to accept that you're with other men—but I think I've made big steps forward. I was doing well on the week-end." He stared at her resolutely, intent on convincing her. "I was totally okay with Derek and Jonas. In fact, I actually found it pretty sexy watching you with them. But when I saw you with Liam and realized . . ." His jaw tensed. "I hadn't been prepared for you to have genuine feelings for someone else. I've been hoping . . . desperately wanting you to want me as the main man in your life. Although I might want things to be different, the only thing that's really important to me is that I'm with you. Loving you. And you loving me. And if I have to share you—not just your body, but your heart, too—then I'm willing to do that."

Before the words could really sink in, he drew her close and captured her mouth again. As his lips moved on hers, her heart swelled. Did he really mean it?

"Sloan, you don't need to share me anymore. I think I'm finally ready to settle down with just one man—and that man is you."

The uncertainty in his face tore at her heart.

"I am happy to hear that, but I don't think it's fair of me to ask you to change."

"You're not asking me. I'm offering. I want to do everything in my power to make this work."

A huge grin lit up his face. "Just hearing that tells me that I'm the only one who has your heart. Thank you, Janine."

He drew her into his arms and held her tight. When he pulled away, his eyes were filled with heat. "What if I were to tell you now that I've had a taste of your wild side, I'm addicted? I don't want to dial it down sexually. Just the opposite. I want to push the boundaries even further."

She smiled. "You do keep telling me how hot you find it when I'm with the other guys."

"True. And after experiencing all these adventures with you, I think you've ruined me for a regular one-on-one with a woman."

She laughed. She couldn't believe Sloan was not only

willing to make such a huge leap forward, but he was even joking about it.

Or could it be that the follow-the-rules Sloan wasn't so much who he was really meant to be as it was a persona he'd taken on after Ben had died? Maybe Sloan was really more of a free spirit like her, and he simply needed someone to help him let go.

He cupped her cheek. "Janine, I love you so much. Will you give me a chance? Will you help me become the man you want me to be?"

At that, tears prickled at her eyes and she smiled. "Oh, Sloan. You are exactly the man I want you to be." She kissed his lips tenderly. "And I will do everything I can to ensure I show you just how much I love you, too. And how we can share that love with others."

She nuzzled under his chin. "But right now, it's just the two of us here, so I think it's the perfect time for some one-on-one sharing—if you don't think that will be too boring."

"Boring? With you, nothing is ever boring." He grinned. "But I actually have another idea."

He grabbed his phone and tapped several keys, then pocketed the phone again.

She narrowed her eyes. It was an odd time for him to answer a text.

"So what's your idea?" she asked.

He stood up and pulled her to her feet, then his mouth consumed hers. His hands stroked down her back and glided over her butt. Then he squeezed, sending her hormones thrumming. Her breasts swelled as they pressed tight against his solid chest.

A knock sounded at the door. Sloan released her, then

opened the door. Liam stood on the other side. He stepped in, a concerned expression on his face.

"So . . . what's the situation?" he asked, his gaze wandering to Janine.

She blanked her expression and sent Sloan a hidden wink, then turned to Liam.

"Well, I'm interviewing for a male harem. You two are my top two candidates. Are you up for it?"

He glanced to Sloan, who couldn't hide his broad grin. Liam's mouth curled in a grin, too.

"Well, not yet, but I will be."

He strode to her and dragged her into his arms, then kissed her until she was breathless. She felt Sloan move behind her and his hands wrap around her waist. His lips found her neck and he nuzzled.

She slipped out from between them and backed toward the couch, then sat down, smiling. "Let me see what you've got."

Both men unzipped their trousers, then dropped them to the floor. Liam's impressive cock, already rising, pushed out from his boxers, which Liam pushed down to his ankles and stepped out of. Sloan's even bigger cock jutted straight up. She wrapped her hand around it and stroked, then tugged on the elastic of his boxers and pulled them down. He kicked them away.

Now both men stood in front of her, naked from the waist down, their two big cocks sticking straight up.

"Well, you certainly both have impressive equipment." She wrapped a hand around each of them and stroked.

She leaned forward and licked Liam from root to tip, then did the same to Sloan. She stroked Sloan up and down while she licked Liam again, then glided her lips around him, sucking his cockhead into her mouth. She swirled her tongue around the tip, then sucked and squeezed until he groaned. She released him and lapped at Sloan's cockhead, then swallowed him into her mouth. The large, mushroom shape filled her mouth. She sucked Sloan as she stroked Liam.

She released them both, then sashayed toward the bedroom, shedding her shirt as she walked. The two men hurried after her. As soon as her shirt slipped to the floor, one of the men unfastened her bra, and both tugged a strap from her shoulder. She slipped the bra off and tossed it aside, then knelt on the bed facing them and cupped her breasts, lifting them as if offering them to the men. Her thumbs stroked over her rigid nipples. The men's gazes heated with lust.

She watched hungrily as Sloan unbuttoned his shirt, revealing hard, muscular flesh beneath. He dropped the garment down his shoulders, then to the floor. She licked her lips at the sight of his big, muscular, naked body. Liam shed his shirt as Sloan knelt on the bed and grabbed her wrist, then pressed the palm to his mouth as he stroked her breast. Liam sat down and stroked her other breast. The feel of two masculine hands on her, stroking her with different pressure and style, set her body aflame. Liam licked her nipple, and she glided her fingers through his short, sandy hair, pulling him to her. Sloan captured her other nipple and sucked. She sighed at the delightful feel of two mouths on her.

Sloan grabbed her other wrist, tugging her hand from Liam's head, then guided her with him to the head of the bed and pulled her onto his cross-legged lap, facing her toward Liam. He held her hands trapped at her sides while Liam grinned, then feasted on her breasts. His tongue swirled over one hard nipple, then the other. He covered one with his mouth and sucked on it. Deep. The pressure sent sensations spiking through her, and she moaned. She melted back against Sloan.

Liam kissed downward, past her navel, then grasped her knees and pressed them wide. His lips teased downward, past her golden star-shaped curls. When his tongue lapped against her clit, she sucked in air. Pleasure quivered through her.

Sloan released her wrists and covered her breasts, squeezing and stroking as Liam teased her sensitive nub with his tongue and his fingertips found her slick opening and glided along it. His finger slipped inside and he stroked her inner passage.

Sloan nuzzled her neck. His hard cock pressed into her back and she reached between them to stroke him. Then she wrapped her hand around him. Liam grasped her legs and drew her down the bed, until her head rested in Sloan's lap. She turned her head and grasped Sloan's big cock and took it in her mouth. She could glide only a little below his cockhead at this angle, so she wrapped her hands around his thick member and stroked while she sucked and squeezed him. Sloan stroked her long hair back from her face as Liam stroked her inside, his tongue flicking on her clit.

Liam sucked, and wild sensations shimmied through her. Sloan caressed her breasts, then tweaked a nipple, and Janine gasped. Liam stroked her inside as he vibrated his tongue on her clit. Her fingers spiked through his hair as her body shuddered. She gasped as an orgasm washed over her.

Liam smiled at her as he prowled up beside her. She smiled back, then rolled over and knelt in front of Sloan.

"That was great, but"—she wrapped a hand around each of their hard cocks—"now it's time for a doubleheader."

She leaned forward and kissed Sloan. Liam knelt behind

her, and she felt his hard erection glide between her thighs. He pressed to her slick opening and slid into her vagina. Her eyelids fell closed as she enjoyed the sensation of his hard shaft gliding into her several times. Then he pressed against her back opening. She pushed her inner muscles to open for him, and he slid into her, his big cock stretching her tight passage.

Sloan gazed at her with intense blue eyes. "It is so sexy watching you while Liam pushes inside you."

He wrapped his hand around his own cock and pressed it to her front opening. Slowly she eased forward, taking him inside her. His huge, thick cock filled her. Slowly. Gliding inside. Penetrating her deeply.

When he was finally fully immersed in her, she drew in a deep breath, enjoying the feel of her two men filling her so wonderfully.

"You like having us both inside you, don't you?" Sloan asked.

"Oh, God, yes." She leaned forward and kissed him. "Now, would you both please fuck me?"

Liam chuckled and wrapped his hands around her hips, holding her tight against his body. Liam drew back, taking her with him. Sloan's cock caressed her insides as it moved out. Then Liam pushed forward, driving Sloan's cock into her again. She squeezed Liam inside her as he oscillated forward and back, thrusting Sloan's cock in and out. It was as if Liam were fucking Sloan through her. Plus, she got the benefits of both hard cocks filling her so deeply.

As Liam continued driving Sloan's cock into her, intense pleasure shuddered through her. She clung to Sloan's shoulders, concentrating on his riveting blue eyes as the cocks filled her and joyful sensations rippled through her.

"Oh, God, you're both making me . . ." She gasped, then moaned. "Oh, you're making me"—her hands tightened around Sloan's shoulders—"come."

She cried out as she rode the wave of ecstasy, compressed between her two men. They stiffened and groaned as one as they climaxed with her.

Finally, they all fell back on the bed, sighing in satisfaction, their limbs tangled together. Sloan tugged her against his body, facing him, and Liam snuggled up behind her.

She smiled in total contentment. This felt so right. There might still be hurdles ahead, but she knew in her heart they would absolutely find a way to make it all work.

Janine gazed at Derek across the table as she told him their news.

Liam and Sloan sat on either side of her at the round table in the outdoor riverside café that she frequented with Derek.

"So you and Sloan are moving into a committed relationship. That's great." Derek smiled at her warmly. "I'm really happy for you."

"And we're hoping you and Liam will still join us, just like always," she said. "Jonas, too, when he's in town."

He glanced at Sloan, who nodded.

Derek's grin broadened. "That's an invitation I sure won't turn down."

Liam chuckled. "Smart man."

"Now, at the risk of being tossed out as a troublemaker, may I make an observation?" Derek asked.

Janine's eyebrows arched. "Sure. What is it?"

"Well, the gender dynamic seems to be wildly out of

balance." He sent her a devilish grin. "I'm thinking maybe there should be another woman in the mix."

Sloan grinned and settled back in his chair. "Actually, that's a great idea."

Liam chuckled. "I'm game."

Janine gazed from one smiling masculine face to another. All their gazes rested on her, waiting for her response.

Watching Liam and Derek make love to another woman . . . Watching *Sloan* make love to another woman . . . How did she feel about that?

She narrowed her eyes and gazed at each man in turn. "Another woman? Hmm." She drummed her fingers on the table absently, as if carefully considering the suggestion. Finally, she leaned back in her chair, folding her arms in front of her. "Well, you know what I think about that?"

Sloan nodded, looking wistful. "I'm pretty sure."

She allowed a slow smile to spread across her face. "I think it's an exceptional idea."

Sloan's eyes widened. "Really?"

She had to stifle a giggle at his shocked expression. "Sure. I think it would be incredibly hot."

Derek chuckled. "Sloan, this woman is going to keep you off balance constantly. Are you sure you can handle it?"

Sloan's arm curled around her waist and he tugged her tight to his body, then captured her lips in a firm kiss.

"Not only will I handle it"—Sloan grinned at her, melting her heart—"I'm going to love every minute of it."

She smiled back at him, joy swelling through her. So would she!

Sizzling erotic romances from OPAL CAREW...

TWIN FANTASIES

SWING

BLUSH

SIX

SECRET TIES

FORBIDDEN HEAT

BLISS
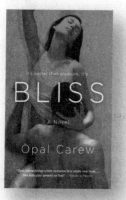

PLEASURE BOUND

TOTAL ABANDON

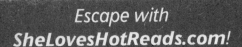